WINNING GLORY

MILITARY ROMANCE — WITH A SCIENCE FICTION EDGE

ANN GIMPEL

Edited by
JENNIFER HASSANI
Illustrated by
FIONA JAYDE

CONTENTS

WINNING GLORY

GENTECH REBELLION, BOOK ONE

Military Romance
(with a science fiction edge)
By
Ann Gimpel

BOOK DESCRIPTION: WINNING GLORY

After years as a black ops CIA agent, nothing surprises Roy Kincaid, yet his current assignment is close to a bust. How could his target—renegade genetic freaks—drop off the radar as if they never existed? Burnt out and discouraged, he hunches over a meal in a backwater diner when a half-frozen woman with the look of an abused runaway staggers through the door. On his feet in an instant, Roy kicks himself. His first instinct is to help her, make certain she stays long enough for the bluish cast to leave her lips. His second is to finish his meal and leave. The world is full of broken women. It's not his job to fix them, but he can't take his eyes off her.

Glory's telepathic ability blares a harsh warning. Roy hunts those like her, but damn if he didn't buy her dinner. Maybe she can fool him, just for tonight. Add a dry motel room to the meal. If she plays it very cool, he'll never find out she's on the run from the same group he's targeted for death.

Enhanced genetics only go so far. A roadblock and her face on a *Most Wanted* flyer shatter her fragile truce with Roy. If her Handlers find her, they'll kill her. If Roy finds out what she is, she'll be worse than dead.

Series Backstory:

Sometime between the interminable wars in the Middle East and 9/11, the United States moved forward breeding a race of super humans. Clandestine labs formed, armed with eager scientists who'd always yearned to manipulate human DNA. At first the clones looked promising, growing to fighting size in as little as a dozen years, but V1 had design flaws.

Seven years ago, a rogue group turned on their creators, blew up the lab, and hit all the other breeding farms, freeing whomever they could find. In the intervening time, they've retreated to hidden compounds and created a society run by men. Women are kept on a tight leash because the men fear if they discover their innate power, they'd launch their own rebellion.

CHAPTER 1

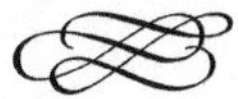

Shadows surrounded Glory. The darkness provided some shielding, but she wanted more—lots more. Too bad invisibility wasn't an option. Her pulse thudded against her eardrums. Sweat formed a banner across her forehead and dripped into her eyes. They stung, and she cursed her human genetic base. When she'd been designed, why the hell hadn't they deep-sixed the annoying things like sweat and fear?

"Get moving!" Her Handler's voice pounded through her head, projected telepathically.

She started. In the midst of her ambivalence, she'd forgotten about the Handlers—also called Nameless Ones—lurking just outside her work area. This was her first real assignment, and they didn't trust her by herself. She blew out a wry breath. They'd probably never trust her, but she was useful.

A low growl followed the Handler's terse words. She scowled as the noise scraped across her preternaturally sharp senses. Glory wanted to balk, make a break for freedom, but it'd be pointless. They'd be on her so fast, she'd be lucky to buy herself an hour.

She gazed straight ahead, assessing her objective. The large office building in downtown Seattle's business district wasn't as deserted as she'd hoped. Lights shone from about a quarter of its windows. If she were fortunate, her target would be unoccupied, but she knew what to say if it wasn't.

No, I know what to do... Talking wasn't exactly on the table.

She sucked in a ragged breath, blew it out, and did it again. Her hair was pulled into a bun, its weight heavy on her neck, but at least it wouldn't come loose and obscure her vision if she had to move quickly.

The growl came again, and she shot forward, trying to walk as if she had every right to be on Pine Street at eleven at night. Unfamiliar high heels lent her an awkward rolling gait, and she pulled her skirt a little higher, so she could adjust her stride. When she'd complained about the black wool business suit and heels, she'd been told she had to look the part if she ran into anyone. She'd have practiced walking in the unfamiliar shoes, but the entire outfit had materialized—dropped in her dorm by a Handler—half an hour before she left her compound.

She fumbled a key card from her suit pocket with damp fingers and swiped it through a reader next to huge, double glass doors that opened onto a lavishly furnished lobby. Pink, white, and purple orchids, plush leather furniture, and glistening gray marble floors felt overwhelming after her spartan existence. After a pause that felt far too long, the scanner's red lights shifted to green, and the door's locking mechanism snicked softly.

Glory darted forward and felt a rush of air as the door swooshed shut behind her. She'd have to use the card to get out too, so she glanced sidelong to identify the reader's location on the lobby side. For long moments, she didn't see a thing, and her already rapid heart rate escalated, making her dizzy.

Doesn't matter. Head for the elevators. I can turn and look better from there.

A creaky grating stopped her cold, until an older, dark-skinned man dressed in a navy blue uniform came into view. He pushed a wheeled bucket with a mop sticking out of it. "Evening, ma'am." He dipped his chin toward her. "Late to be working, isn't it?"

She nodded. "I, uh, I forgot something I needed."

He nodded back. "Always something, eh?" His smile displayed several missing teeth; grizzled gray hair lay flat against his head.

Because she was too keyed up to talk, and finding words was hard, she trotted toward the elevator, nearly twisting an ankle in the process from her sleek, black pumps. She still had the electronic card in hand. The Nameless Ones had done reconnaissance and funneled needed data into her processing unit. It was how she knew she'd need the key card to call the elevator after hours—and everything else about this assignment.

She swiped the card and pushed the up button. Somewhere above her, machinery whirred. She wanted to look back at the front door, but self-preservation and not attracting attention trumped everything.

The housekeeper whistled as he drew his mop across the shiny floor. She listened, trying to make out the tune, but it wasn't familiar. The elevator doors opened, and she stepped inside, turning as she did to catch a glimpse of the electronic scanner that had to be near the front door.

Breath rattled from her constricted lungs. There it was. About a foot to the right of the door, which was why she hadn't noticed it before. Excellent. Her egress—assuming she made it that far— would be smooth, rather than awkward. It'd look suspicious if she had no idea how to exit the building. Floors whooshed past, and she got out on the fourteenth. Squaring her shoulders, she took advantage of her almost six-foot height to project the illusion she belonged here, in the center of corporate America late at night.

This building in the heart of Seattle was as close to the Silicon Valley as the Northwest got. Many major hardware and software manufacturers had offices here, but she was only focused on one of them—Dynamic Solutions. DS was deeply involved in government contracting for classified genetic research. The Handlers told her that much, but nothing further, and she'd known better than to ask.

Her heels beat a staccato on green-veined, creamy marble as she made her way to the end of the hall. She traded the key card still clutched in her sweaty hand for a different one, swiped it, and slipped on transparent latex gloves before letting herself into a mercifully dark suite of offices.

Get what I came for and leave, ran through her mind like a mantra. The cleanup person had seen her, but he wouldn't be a problem, not so long as everything else went smoothly. Her heart still beat too fast, and she was sweating despite the cool November evening and the sixty degree temperature in the building, but so far so good.

The office layout was exactly what she'd seen in schematics. She strode purposively toward a corner office. The door was shut and she twisted the latch.

It didn't turn.

Goddammit! Locked. What do I do now? A perverse part of her thrilled because the Nameless Ones' intel had flaws. She hated them so much, any evidence of their weakness meant maybe she could escape someday.

Her practical side intruded, and she looked for a keycard slot in the door. Picking locks was easy; it wouldn't slow her down much. When she didn't find one, she hunted for an electronic device and groaned when she saw a retinal scanner. She could defeat it, but she needed permission to break protocol, plus she didn't want to kick off the building's alarm system if there was a way around it.

"There's a retinal scanner," she sent telepathically to her Handlers.

"Break the lock."

"But that will set off alarms," she protested. Her thin, silk blouse stuck to her, and she pulled it away from her breasts, hoping to dry her damp skin.

"Give us credit for something," the voice snarled. *"We disabled them.*

Hurry. We don't have all night." After a pause, he added, *"Speed is your friend."*

Glory stared at the door. She could open the lock with her mind. It wouldn't be hard. Had the Nameless One lied to her about the alarms? They certainly weren't beyond that, but if she couldn't believe them, it made every shred of intel supporting this mission suspect. She closed her teeth over her bottom lip so hard she tasted blood. She had to do something. Fish or cut bait.

If she left empty handed, there'd be hell to pay. Time in a cell to contemplate her failure. She shook herself to force her body into action. It had been a long road to get where she was right now, earning enough of the Nameless Ones' trust to be allowed out of the compound. She might never regain the ground she lost if she jack-rabbited out of here with her tail between her legs.

Fuck it.

She called the power that flowed through her mind. Electricity crackled from her fingertips, forcing the retinal scanner's hand, and the door sprang open. Doubts that had dogged her ever since she stood outside plotting her course of action vanished. She vaulted through the door, kicked it shut, and dove into a black leather chair sitting behind an enormous mahogany desk. She flipped switches, activating the computer and movie-sized flat screen monitor.

"Come on," she urged under her breath, fingers poised over a keyboard. A box flashed onto the screen requesting username and password information. She typed what she'd been told—and got an error message. Glory typed it again. Same message.

What the hell?

One explanation jumped to the top of the heap. The computer's owner must have changed it after the Nameless Ones infiltrated this company. She didn't hesitate. Assuming the username would be the same, she typed it and then created anagrams from the password in every permutation and combination. The process was quick, because her brain was just like the computer she was hacking into.

With her fingers moving so fast they were a blur, she blended her consciousness with the CPU droning at her feet. When it wanted to shut down and sound an alarm after three tries to access its secrets, she reached deep enough into its operating system code to stymie the automatic rejection sequence and bypass the password entirely.

"Yes!" Glory fist pumped the air when menus rolled across the screen. She yanked a flash drive from her skirt pocket, slotted it into a USB port, and started the download, selecting files as she went. She covered her electronic presence so well that if she wasn't disturbed, no one would ever know she'd been here. The company had safeguards to keep her from breaking in from an external computer, but they couldn't keep her out when she was logged in from one of their own.

She wondered how the Nameless Ones acquired the username and worthless password, but they never told her things like that. They'd probably borrowed data from one of those software programs where the unwary store all their important data—never realizing how easy they are to hack. Or installed a keystroke logger. She smiled wryly. What a bunch of rubes humans were. If she ever escaped the Nameless Ones, blending in shouldn't be too hard.

When the drive filled, she inserted another and then two more.

Her fingers skimmed the keyboard as file after file dropped into her drives. Only one more drive and she'd be done. There. Glory pocketed her flash drives, four in all, and shut the machine down. She'd just gotten up from the chair when she heard the outer office door open. Thank Christ she hadn't turned on any lights. Floor to ceiling curtains partially shrouded windows that looked out on a busy waterfront. She raced behind one and arranged it to hide her.

Barely breathing, she waited, shifting from foot to foot. Glory rode herd on her nerves and forced stillness, concentrating hard to alter reality. It wasn't a skill she was good at since the Handlers didn't encourage its use.

Fuck! Go away so I can leave.

An unpleasant whirring clawed at her sensitive hearing as the retinal scanner did its work and allowed access to whoever was standing outside. So much for altering reality to suit her needs.

"I'll just be a minute," a man's voice spoke, and he clumped through the door.

"Work, work, work," a woman groused. "You promised tonight would be just us, and here we are back at your goddamned office."

The heavy footsteps paused. "This *goddamned office* supports you," the man said, his tone heavy with bitterness.

Clearly, this was an old bone of contention between the couple. While she'd never lived around humans, Glory watched plenty of television, and she spent hours each day on the Internet.

She took shallow breaths. Her nose tickled, but she pinched it to avoid sneezing. It didn't look as if the man and his partner would be here long. The footsteps started again and then stopped.

"That's odd," the man said.

Glory's heart jumped into hyper drive. What hadn't she done? Was it the chair? Had she left it wrong, somehow? Who the fuck recalled exactly how they left their chair anyway?

"What's odd?" Lighter steps, wearing heels.

"I always push my chair in when I leave. It's been moved."

"Oh for Christ's sake, Lloyd. That high-clearance cleaning staff you were going on about the other day must've moved it. Let's go."

"Mmph. You're probably right."

A desk drawer opened and closed, followed by another. More steps as the couple left, door shutting behind them.

Glory didn't breathe normally until the door closed. She counted to five hundred very slowly before she left her hiding place and exited the office. Even though it should be enough time, she remained frightened she'd run into Lloyd and his grumpy companion. Once she was in the corridor leading to the elevator at the end of the fourteenth floor, she started to relax.

I did it.

Not yet. I'm not out yet.

She rode the elevator down and made her way to the outside door. The janitor was nowhere in sight, and the door's scanner flashed green as soon as she swiped her key card. The chill damp of a Seattle night felt like a balm on her overheated skin, and she walked briskly toward the pickup point two blocks away. The shoes didn't bother her as much. Maybe she was getting used to them.

Nothing could go wrong now. She was in the clear. She had what she came for. Glory snaked a hand into her pocket and cradled the drives. She'd memorized the file names driving here, but they were in some kind of code that didn't make sense, even when she ran it through her augmented brain. She'd been instructed not to take time to read any of what she'd stolen. Good thing she didn't break protocol. As it was, she escaped detection by a very narrow margin. A few more seconds downloading, and Lloyd would've caught her in the act.

Breath hissed through her teeth, and her stomach clenched. If Lloyd had waltzed in before she shut the computer off, he'd have turned his office upside down hunting for an intruder, given how spun out he was about his fucking chair. She shook her head. Her instructions were to kill if she were apprehended. A quick blast to melt neurons into mush. Not that she hadn't practiced with dummies, but she'd never actually harmed a living creature. When it got right down to it, she wasn't certain she could.

"It's about time." A man dressed in black sidled next to her from the maw of a nearby alleyway.

"Did you get it?" A second man, similarly dressed, joined the first. Both were tall, close to six feet four, with shaggy dark hair and heavily muscled bodies. They always wore dark glasses, even indoors, so she had no idea what their eyes looked like. The men were genetically altered, just like her. One of the government's many experiments that had leaped its boundaries, gone sideways, and produced freaks that had to be hidden away from polite society.

The thought brought a smile to her lips, and the second man

slugged her in the arm. "Look at her. Grinning like a shit-eating demon. Of course she got it."

"Almost didn't," she said. "The man who works in that office came back."

The first man turned her head toward her and furled his brows. "And?"

"I didn't have to do anything. I hid behind a curtain until he left."

"Excellent." The man blew out a tense breath.

"Yeah," the other man seconded. "Always better when we don't have to send in the drones to clean up."

Glory hurried to keep up with them. She'd never heard this part before. "So someone would have shown up to get rid of the bodies?"

"Ssht!" One of the Nameless Ones jabbed her hard with his elbow.

It felt like a steel pipe pounding into her side, and she grunted with pain but understood to keep her mouth shut. They came to a black SUV, and she got into the back seat, rubbing her sore ribs. The men climbed in the front, and the vehicle pulled away from the curb at a sedate pace.

She twisted around and got onto her knees, so she could reach her bundle of clothes behind the rear seat. Once she had them, she faced forward again and dug for her worn black trousers and battered lace up boots. Realizing she still had the clear, latex gloves on, she peeled them off and asked, "Is it okay if I change into my other clothes?" She kicked off the high heels before getting an answer.

"Permission granted." The Nameless One in the passenger seat adjusted the rear view mirror so his gaze met hers. "Mind if I watch?"

It wasn't a question. Not really, so she didn't bother to answer, just pulled on her pants before she slithered out of her skirt. She was damned if she'd give him any more of a peep show than she had to. Because he'd want to humor her, and maybe catch a glimpse of tit, she gathered her courage. "You never answered me about the bodies."

"That's because you asked in a public place." He sounded annoyingly patronizing. "Come on, babe. Aren't you going to take that jacket off? And your blouse?"

She shrugged the jacket off and undid one button, but very slowly. Feeling like she might have the upper hand for once, albeit temporarily, she crooked two fingers and smiled. "Information first."

"You drive a hard bargain." He reached a hand toward his lap. "That's not all that's hard."

The driver shot a glance at his partner. "She's off limits, and you know it."

"Who'd tell?"

"I would," the driver said sourly. He twisted the rear view mirror and looked at her. "We never leave evidence of our missions. If you'd had to terminate anyone, we would've done away with the bodies, and any associated untidiness."

"Thank you for the information." Glory pulled a bulky gray, wool sweater out of her clothes bag and put it on over her cream-colored silk blouse. Because her head ached from the weight of her hair, she pulled the pins holding her bun in place and sheaves of shiny darkness rippled around her.

"Aw, what happened to my tit show?" The Nameless One sounded annoyed.

"It was cancelled." Glory leaned back against the leather seat and exhaled long and loud.

The man in the passenger seat moved so fast, she didn't understand how he could possibly have vaulted over the divider and be seated next to her. The chiseled lines of his face were set into a harsh expression, and he shoved a hand in front of her.

"Give." He opened and closed his fist.

Understanding, she dug into the clothes bag and found the skirt she'd just removed. Glory extracted the flash drives and handed them over. "You can go back to the front seat," she told him.

"Nah, think I'll stay right where I am." He leered at her and patted his lap again.

"I still don't understand why you didn't have me merge with the computer and do a direct download into my brain," she said. "It'd have been much faster." A flash of insight slammed her between the eyes. She could've done both—if she weren't so scared of her Handlers.

"Too much temptation." The man eyed her. "This way, we know you didn't peek."

She smelled his arousal, and it disgusted her. All the Nameless Ones disgusted her. The driver was correct about her being off limits. They left her alone for some unknown reason—or they had until now. Her and the other girls like her. Glory closed her eyes to block out the man next to her. She could still smell him, but at least she didn't have to look at him.

She let her body sag against the seat. It was a long drive back to the compound, well over two hours. Maybe she could catch some sleep. She felt hungry, but asking them to stop at a fast food joint would buy her bupkis. A bottle of water rattled in the door; she made a grab for it, unscrewed the cap, and drained it. At least the Nameless One was keeping his distance. Good. They'd never pawed her before, but there was always a first time.

As miles clicked by, she scrolled what she knew about her origins through her mind. It wasn't much, which was frustrating. It felt as if there was a locked file in her head, just out of reach. If she could only pop the code, everything would become clear.

Yeah, I've been trying to decipher that secret for years.

Sometimes, she got tantalizingly close, only to have truth fritter away in puffs of smoke.

"You'll never figure it out," the man sitting next to her said.

"Gawk! Stay out of my head." She drew as far away from him as she could, hugging the door panel.

"I can't fuck you, but no one said I couldn't rape your thoughts," the man retorted smugly.

Glory ignored him. She withdrew deep into the place in her mind no one could reach and hovered there. Did the ignorant asshole next to her know she could kill him from where she sat without even touching him?

An unpleasant thought intruded. Of course he knew, because he could do the same thing.

CHAPTER 2

*R*oy Kincaid keyed his mic, just a single tap to keep talking at bare minimums per protocol. Answering beeps hummed against his ears, and he counted until he got to six. The team was in place. Good. They could move out. He keyed his mic again to alert his men that they were on the move.

Ahead of them a rattletrap farmhouse peeked from behind dense tree cover. Cottonwoods and aspens grew thickly. The place felt deserted to his artificially enhanced senses, but CIA intel suggested otherwise. Another nest of freaks—genetically engineered humans who'd gone rogue—had been spotted here by The Company's aerial surveillance network.

Roy glanced skyward. Clouds covered most of the stars and a half-grown moon. He'd counted on darkness, and for once Mother Nature was fully cooperative. He glided forward, his thick-soled combat boots making little noise as he used old growth tree boles to shield his body from anyone who might be inside the farmhouse. Freaks always posted sentries, so where were they?

Yeah, good question.

He stopped at the last tree before a stretch of open ground between him and the house and tapped his mic to signal everyone else to stop too. Roy stared at the structure with a gaping hole in the roof. One side was falling in. The wraparound porch sagged, suggesting the place had been deserted for years. A raccoon sashayed out a hole in the front door, paused, and then chirped. Another raccoon joined the first, and they waltzed across the porch and down the stairs, followed by a group of babies.

"What the fuck?" Charlie spoke, breaking protocol, but it didn't matter. If rodents lived inside the house, freaks didn't.

"I have no idea, but let's find out." No longer worried about shielding their presence, Roy strode across the yard along with his men, who fanned around the farmhouse approaching from half a dozen different angles.

Something subtle shifted in the air currents eddying around the house. If Roy hadn't taken the injections to make him more like the freaks they hunted, he'd never have noticed. "Stop!" he barked.

Too late.

An explosion flashed from the rear of the house, followed by gut-wrenching screams as one of his men turned into grisly chunks of protoplasm.

"Fall back," Roy shouted. "To me."

When he did a nose count, Ted came up missing. Roy ground his teeth together. They'd walked into the trap like prime suckers. The freaks had set them up before, just not lately.

"Goddammit!" Charlie sputtered. "If I'd been half a foot closer to Ted, I'd have bought it too."

"Bastards," someone else spat.

Roy moved toward the rear of the building keeping to the tree line. Ted's cries had ceased almost immediately, so the man must be dead, but they had to check if enough of him remained to retrieve for a hero's burial. He clenched his jaw harder. The worst part about leading men on black ops missions was losing them. Despite years in the field, he'd never gotten over the guilt he felt for every single man he'd lost.

'What do you think, boss?" Charlie jerked his chin at a quivering heap of red with slivers of bone sticking out. The raccoons had already closed on the corpse, intent on stripping it.

Roy didn't answer. He picked up a fist sized rock and chucked it at the raccoons, but all they did was hiss at him. Apparently Ted was too succulent a feast to walk away from without putting up a fight. The rock told him whatever explosives were there had been tripped, so he strode forward. The largest raccoon turned and snarled, ready to do battle. Roy kicked it square in the chin; it flew backward and landed with a splat before turning tail and scrambling into a bramble thicket. The rest of the raccoons raced after it.

Mindless of the rivers of blood, Roy hefted what was left of his man and turned toward their vehicles parked half a mile away. The others followed.

"Would you like a hand?" Charlie asked once they'd cleared fencing around the property.

"No point both of us turning into head to toe gore."

As he carted his burden, Roy thought about his thirteen plus years with an entity the U.S. government would never admit existed. Loosely affiliated with the Central Intelligence Agency, his black-ops group took care of everything the CIA couldn't. When he'd first signed on, just out of law school, the job had been easier —much easier. There'd actually been months between assignments. In the interim, he and his hand-picked team worked for The Company, a well-used euphemism for the CIA, doing other things.

That was before a series of top secret government experiments came to light. Sometime between the beginning of the interminable wars in the Middle East and 9/11, the United States decided they needed to breed a race of super humans. Clandestine labs were created, armed with eager scientists who'd always yearned to manipulate human DNA. At first the clones—or whatever they were —looked promising, growing to fighting size in as little as a dozen years.

Seven years ago, a rogue group turned on their creators, blew up the lab, and hit all the other breeding farms, freeing whoever they could find.

Roy shifted the burden across his shoulders and more blood sheeted from the corpse, coating his boots. The last seven years had been hell, no way around it. While occasionally successful, the majority of their efforts to eradicate the freaks ended like today's mission. In an attempt to even the scoreboard, he'd volunteered for a series of injections to augment his abilities. Because it was risky, he'd served as a guinea pig.

Once he determined the mixture really did give him an edge, he insisted his men sign up for it too. The ones who balked ended up with more normal jobs for The Company.

A loud zipping sound snapped Roy's chin up. Charlie had retrieved a body bag from his trunk, and it lay open on the ground. Roy shifted Ted onto it. Charlie zipped him in. Thank fucking God Ted wasn't married. Telling wives was always the worst. For some reason parents came to terms with losing their sons with far less drama.

He looked at his clothes. His black pants, black top, and black gloves were covered in bits of bone, with clumps of tissue here and there. He couldn't get into the car like that. He considered walking back to Langley, but it was better than ten miles. Dawn wasn't far off, and he'd attract attention in his current state.

"Want to change?" One of his men asked. "I put sweats in the back of my car after our last fuck—" He cleared his throat and tried again. "Mission. After our last mission."

Roy sat on the ground next to Ted and laid a hand on the body bag. "I'm sorry, bro." He followed his words with a silent prayer Ted's soul would find the peace that eluded the man in life.

He began untying his boots and looked at David, the man who'd offered sweats. Like all of them, his hair was dyed jet black and his face covered with grease paint. Hard hazel eyes glittered dangerously. They could've been clones, just like the freaks with their lanky, hard-bodied builds. "I'll take you up on those sweats," he said. "And you don't have to pussyfoot around me. Our last assignment was a worse disaster than this one."

He toed off his boots, scrambled upright, and slid out of his pants. "Does anyone have a plastic bag big enough for my gear?"

David nodded. "Yeah, you can use the same bag I put the sweats in."

Roy dressed in silence. He wiped his hands on the cleaner parts of his field clothes before stuffing them into the plastic sack. As he got himself together enough to leave, a plan formed in his mind. He gestured to Charlie, and they hoisted Ted's body bag into one of the car's trunks. They drove separately because two commando-looking men in a car might arouse suspicion, and their cars were as unremarkable as they could manage. Ten year old imports with peeling paint and a few dings and dents. Because the rides were cheap, they traded them out frequently.

He shut the trunk lid gently and turned to his men. "I'm going to float an idea past the mother ship tomorrow morning." He waited, but no one asked anything, almost as if they dreaded their next assignment. Roy didn't blame them. For some reason, the freaks' level of aggression had accelerated dramatically these past few months. If things continued the way they had recently, it was only a matter of time before he and his team were all dead.

He straightened his shoulders. "If I get approval, I'll go deep."

"But we're already black ops." David pointed out.

"Yeah, well I plan to go even deeper. And I'll go alone."

Growls of disapproval rattled from behind five sets of gritted teeth.

"You can't do that, boss," Charlie protested.

"You need us for backup." David stood taller.

"It'd be like signing up for a suicide mission," another man cut in. "Can't let you do that, sir."

"And what we're doing now isn't a suicide mission?" Roy pressed his lips into a hard line. "I don't feel right leading you into any more traps. If it's just me, I have more maneuverability."

"Yeah, but you're more vulnerable too," David argued.

"It'll be a wash." Roy tried for an even tone. "I told you as a courtesy. This isn't up for group discussion."

Charlie drew his brows together into a thick, worried line. "This means we'll go back to the main office." He hesitated a beat. "We can keep our communicators. They run on a closed channel. No one else can pick up our transmissions."

"Except the freaks," David muttered.

"Anyway," Charlie hurried on. "If something goes bad wrong, you radio us. Don't even need to say anything. Just key the mic like you did tonight. We'll get your location from the GPS coordinates and be there as soon as we can."

A murmur of assent swept through the five men standing in front of him, and Roy swallowed hard. Gratitude for their loyalty filled him with pride. He'd chosen well.

"You got it." He flashed a thumbs up sign. "Now let's get back to HQ. We need to let them know about Ted." He picked up the bag with his blood-saturated clothing, chucked it into the backseat of his Toyota Tercel, and got behind the wheel.

CHAPTER 3

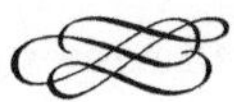

Glory must've dozed off because the car crunching on gravel jolted her to wakefulness. "Home?" She slurred the question and rubbed the back of one hand across her eyes. The hazel contacts that obscured her agate-green eyes, scratched and she drew her hand back.

"Yes, we're back," the driver confirmed. "If you stop by the kitchen, they've been instructed to give you tonight's meal. Once you're done eating, go straight to the dormitory."

"What about these?" She tapped the clothes bag sitting in her lap.

"They're yours. Be sure to hang them up and wash the blouse. It stinks."

"You'll need them for your next assignment," the Nameless One next to her, cut in.

Glory scrambled out of the car and loped toward an open door at the end of the long, low concrete barracks. The Nameless One standing guard duty at the well-lit entrance gave her a curt nod. It seemed he might actually speak to her, but the moment passed, and he didn't. It was rare for the men to engage in unnecessary conversation.

She gloried in the feel of her flat boot soles slapping the gray stone floor of the bunker she'd called home for as long as she could remember. Whoever invented high heels should be strung up by their thumbs. The building had three wings, a long central one and two side structures. The square between them housed the gym and arena. Glory wasn't certain how many people lived here because she only interacted with the dozen girls in her dormitory and a few of the Nameless Ones.

She and the girls hadn't had names either, until about a year ago when they'd gotten sick of being called by numbers and named themselves. Glory smothered a grin. Names had been their first power gambit, and they'd insisted the Handlers use them by not responding anymore when their numbers were called. There'd been a few beatings, but she and the girls held firm. And they'd won. Victory was sweet, since it was the first she remembered.

Glory ducked into the dimly-lit kitchen. A plate sat atop one of the huge, stainless steel ranges. She grabbed it, rustled a fork from a drawer, and stuffed food into her mouth standing over her plate. Food wasn't allowed in the rooms, so she'd have to finish this here, but as hungry as she was, she inhaled the meat and vegetable stew, slathered butter on the roll, and ate it too. She still felt half-starved when the plate was empty. Hoping the chillers weren't locked, she tried them without any luck. As a consolation prize, she turned the cold water tap on, cupped her hands under it, and drank her fill.

She turned away and picked up her clothes bag, intent on the dormitory and her hard, single bed. A thought almost blinded her, and she moved in front of one of the stainless steel chiller doors again. If she could open that office door tonight, surely she could force the lock on the chiller.

She was practically shredding the plastic bag that held her clothing and willed her hands to relax. Yes, she could force the door, but punishment would be swift. No one would doubt who'd been here, since she was the only one awake—aside from Nameless Ones, and they got to eat whatever they wanted.

She balled her hands into fists again. Someday, she'd have

whatever she wanted to eat too, but not tonight. Tonight, she needed sleep. Suddenly weary, she plodded out of the kitchen and down the long corridor to the dormitory where she lived when she wasn't in a punishment cell. She walked mindlessly, her thoughts wandering.

The compound was tucked in a confusing welter of logging roads between Seattle and the Cascade Mountains, which ran down the center of Washington State. She'd found it on Google Earth, but the buildings were nearly hidden by a thick evergreen forest. If she hadn't known about the compound, she'd never have seen telltale signs of it on the mapping software. She'd heard rumors it was originally a bunker left over from when the U.S. had been gearing up for an atomic threat from the Middle East.

Regardless, her home was definitely a no-frills environment. Built of concrete blocks, the bunker was hot in the summer and cold through the winters. The girls were allowed small, electric heaters in the dorms, but if too many used them at once, circuits blew. She thought back, trying to remember her life before this place. Surely, she'd had a life. She'd been around thirteen, maybe as much as fourteen or fifteen, when she was dropped off here. Just past puberty, getting breasts and her first period.

Like every other time she tried to remember, something blocked her, and a vague headache pounded behind her temples. She and the other girls she arrived with tried lots of things to push past the barrier in their minds, but they never had any success. Once the Handlers figured out what they were doing, they were put on short rations for a month and locked in punishment cells.

She exhaled bitterly and instructed herself to think about other things. She was too tired right now to figure anything out. She laid her palm across a glass plate next to the dormitory's door, and it opened to her touch. The bunker might not have frills to make her life cushier, but it was sure high tech. While the Handlers rationed her food, they never complained about her long hours on the Internet learning about the world beyond the compound.

Makes sense. I'm more like the computers than a person anyway. So are the men.

After dropping her clothes bag on top of her dresser, she made her way to her bunk and sat on the edge to take off her boots. She'd hang the clothes up tomorrow—and rinse out the blouse. Even though she tried to be silent, shadows closed from both sides. Hope and Charity settled, one on each side of her.

"How'd it go?" Hope whispered.

"Fine."

"Were you scared?" Charity also kept her voice low.

Glory considered lying, but gave it up. Her friends would know. Picking out a particular tonal quality in speech that meant someone wasn't telling the truth was one of their gifts. "Petrified," she murmured. "You guys should go back to bed. Sometimes the Nameless Ones look in on us."

As if her words were prophetic, the dormitory door slammed open. Lights flared; she blinked against the sudden intrusion. Her stomach tightened, and the meal she'd just eaten curdled in her gut.

Three Nameless Ones tromped into the dormitory. "Taking up a gay lifestyle, girls?" one inquired archly.

"We think you should reconsider," another said.

Glory shot to her feet. "You can't touch us," she snarled.

Hope and Charity flanked her. "We're off limits," Hope growled.

"If you're so off limits, you ought to wear more to bed." The third Nameless One, another hard-bodied man with sunglasses and unkempt dark hair jerked a chin at the thin T-shirts barely covering the girls' private parts.

"It's not like we were expecting company." Charity tossed her head.

"If you don't want company, don't break the rules," the first man said, following it with, "Lights out means—"

"We know exactly what it means," Glory interrupted, wondering where her burst of courage came from.

"No, babe, you don't." A fourth Nameless One entered the room and shoved the door shut behind him.

Glory groaned. It was the same Handler who'd shared the back seat with her on the ride back. She glanced around the room. The other girls were frozen in their bunks, turned away, or pretending to be dead. She padded right in front of man, crossed her arms beneath her breasts, and met his sunglass covered eyes in silent challenge.

"Decided you like me?" he smirked.

"No, but this is between us. Leave them out of it." She swept her arms wide to encompass her roommates.

"Between you and me, eh? I like the sound of that." He extended a hand, but Glory ignored it. He eyed the other Handlers. "You can leave, boys. I've got this under control."

"Whatever you say, buddy," one of the Nameless Ones muttered, spun on his heel, and pulled the door open. The other two followed him. Booted footsteps echoed down the stone-floored hall beyond the door.

"So long as they left the door open, shall we follow them?" The Nameless One standing toe to toe with her shot out a hand and gripped her upper arm.

"Let me get my slippers. The floor's cold."

He nodded once and let her go.

Hope's and Charity's clear, green eyes mirrored despair. Glory motioned them back to their bunks. No point in giving the Handler an opportunity to tap all three of them for whatever sexual escapade he had in mind. She fished a worn pair of running shoes that doubled as slippers from beneath her bunk and stuffed her stocking-clad feet into them, bending to drag the heels on. Thank God, she'd only taken off her boots. The sooner she could get lover boy away from a potential orgy, the better.

The lust smell rolled off him in waves that brought bile shooting into the back of her throat. "Lead out," she managed through clenched teeth.

He gripped her upper arm again, as if he expected her to take off the second she had a clear corridor to run down, and marched her out of the dorm. Camera eyes lined the juncture where the wall met the ceiling. Glory hoped someone was watching—and listening. "I don't want to go with you," she spoke clearly and louder than she had to. "But I don't want you to hurt my friends, either."

"Shut up," he hissed, having divined her intent.

Glory didn't give up. "What?" She shot a predatory smile his way. "You don't want your buddies to know you're about to break a cardinal rule?"

"I'm escorting you to a cell." He smiled back. Showed a mouthful of teeth, anyway. It didn't feel much like a smile.

"Like hell you are, pal." She jerked her thumb behind her. "The cells are the other way."

"We built new ones. Just for you." He lowered his head until his mouth hovered over her ear. "This won't take long, sweetheart. Be a good girl and cooperate. If you do, I'll see you get double rations next week."

She glanced at the tented out front of his pants. Even though she'd never gotten close enough to a man for any sort of intimacy, she understood the mechanics of sex well enough. All the girls did. They talked about imaginary lovers and stroked themselves to orgasm after lights out.

Thoughts crowded one another as she formed and discarded plans. Because her mind was faster than any processing unit, she balanced the pros and cons of many scenarios simultaneously. Only a single viable course of action popped up. It was dangerous, and sooner than she'd planned, but the Nameless One was forcing her hand.

"The longer we stand here in the hall," she murmured, "the more risky this is."

Something in his posture relaxed fractionally as he took her words to mean she'd give him what he wanted. He shifted his grip on her, and she felt mind power flow from him as the camera eyes turned up in their swivel sockets. Glory filed that trick away. It meant no one could see them, and by the time another Nameless One came to investigate, they'd be out of range.

Maybe she could get something else useful out of him before this played itself out. *"Where'd we come from?"* She used mental speech, shielding it as she'd been taught.

"What do you mean?" He led her down a side hallway she'd never taken before.

"Where was I before I ended up here?"

He shrugged. *"You girls came from different labs."*

She stumbled slightly, but his grip kept her upright. Labs. She came from a lab, not a home. She'd suspected as much, but it still hurt to hear it. *Figures. It's why I can do all that stuff.*

"Were we born in labs? Like test-tube babies?" She pressed since he was in a talking mood.

He laid his palm on a glass plate next to a door, and it swung open. He half pushed, half dragged her inside. Glory's mouth gaped open. The room was obviously just for him since it contained one bed pushed into a corner. A sofa with floral upholstery fronted a low table loaded with books. Off to one side, a computer desk held a computer and monitor. The room even had a window and fresh, cold air streamed inside.

"Is it safe to talk in here?" He nodded, and she went on, "Then you can answer me."

"No, I can't. Or I could, but I won't. The less you girls know the better."

"How come you get to know things, and I don't?"

He let go of her and took off his dark glasses. She stared at amber cat eyes with a vertical slit pupil. At least that explained why the Nameless Ones never took their shades off. "Do all of you have the same eyes?"

"What do you think?" He stroked a hand down the side of her face.

"Probably, since the girls' eyes are the same."

"You might be right." He pulled her against her body and she felt his cock press into her belly. He groaned and thrust against her.

"You never answered me about the labs we came from."

"And I'm not going to. If things work out between us, maybe I'll tell you more."

He dropped his hands to her butt, increasing the contact between their bodies. She turned her face up, and he closed his mouth over hers. Snaking out a thread of power, she linked to his mind, keeping her touch light, subtle. He was so sunk in wanting her, he'd never notice. She hoped. He ground his pelvis against her, his breath coming fast as he jammed his tongue inside her mouth.

When he started pawing at her clothes, trying to get them out of the way, she took advantage of the passageway she'd established into his mind and hurled the highest voltage she had through it. His body jerked spasmodically, and he fell to the floor. She pushed more power after the first jolt until she was certain he was dead.

Shit. Crap. Fuck. I killed someone.

He deserved it. He was going to rape me.

Got to get out of here.

Heart pounding, she gauged the window's opening. It was barely big enough, but if she went through head first, she was pretty sure she could establish enough momentum to get outside. For a long, thundering moment, she stood and stared at the first person she'd ever killed. Guilt knifed through her, but she shoved it deep. There'd be time to examine her feelings later—if she escaped.

What she had here wasn't any sort of life. She and the girls had fantasized escaping hundreds of times.

Get moving. Now.

She mirrored her thoughts from earlier that evening and flew across the room. The window opening was bigger than it looked, and she ended up sprawled face down in wet earth. Glory scrambled to her feet and faded into thick foliage surrounding the compound. If she knew how to drive, she'd filch a car, but for her to guess at this skill would bring her to someone's attention much faster than she wanted.

At least the Nameless Ones couldn't alert any other authorities, but they could look for her. And they would. Once they discovered one of them was dead and she was missing, they'd track her with the single-minded intensity of a starving lion closing on prey.

"One thing at a time," she muttered under her breath. "I've got to find somewhere I can hide before the sun comes up, and they can find me from the air."

She had at least three hours before anyone would come after her. No one would discover her absence until the five a.m. alarm. Likely no one would come looking for the Nameless One lying in his room before that, either. Of course they wouldn't. The other men would cover for him since they thought he was having it off with her. Tossing stealth to the winds in favor of speed, she tapped her augmented strength to run faster and headed for the place asphalt turned to gravel at the turnoff to the compound. Once there, she kept running until she hit a large feeder road. This road usually had traffic, but it would be a neat trick to snag a ride in the middle of the night.

Please. She bent her mind to shape events. *Let a car come by and pick me up.*

Headlights flickered far up the way. She slowed to a walk and stuck out her thumb, smothering a satisfied smile. She'd practiced using her thoughts to create new realities, but it hadn't worked to keep Lloyd out of his office earlier tonight. Having something work in the lab at the compound and out here in the real world were two different things.

A late model blue pickup truck skidded to a halt next to her. A middle-aged man leaned out his window. He wore a cowboy hat and had a genuinely nice smile. "Need a ride, miss?"

"I sure do." She smiled back.

"Where you going?"

She met his rheumy, blue eyes, and sent encouraging thoughts his way. "As far away from here as I can get."

"I understand. Been there myself a time or two. Come on. Get in."

Glory walked around the truck and climbed into the high cab. "Thanks very much," she said as the truck rolled down the road into darkness. "I was afraid no one would stop."

"You're welcome. I'm Clive. What's your name?"

Such a simple question, but one she'd never been asked before. "Glory. My name is Glory."

"Well, Miss Glory. We got us some time. Suppose you tell me how you came to be walking by the side of a deserted highway in the middle of the night."

Whatever story she came up with would be one she'd use again and again. Easier that way than sorting through an ever-changing tangle of lies. Glory opened her mouth to fabricate a life that had never been and let her creativity roll.

CHAPTER 4

Roy sat in a nondescript café, hunched over a cup of steaming, black coffee, warming his hands on the thick, white ceramic mug. Three weeks had passed since he'd made the decision to go it alone. The first week was eaten up in endless meetings with his superiors in the CIA. They'd argued against his course of action, but in the end, they relented. They'd had to. No one with half a brain could argue they were winning this war.

One of the problems was no one knew exactly what the freaks could do—the full extent of their powers—or even if they all had the same abilities. The scientists who weren't killed during the rebellion seven years before had fled, going even deeper underground than Roy. Obviously, they didn't trust the government to keep them safe, and they'd taken matters in hand. A fresh group of scientists were working on the problem, but without information from the initial crew, it was slow going.

Roy had a list of names and last known locations of the original scientists, who might still be alive. It was where he'd decided to start. If he could uncover even one of the men or women who'd created the monstrosities threatening them—and if he could get them to talk with him, which was a huge unknown—it would make his job much easier.

As things stood, he had nothing. No scientists. No freaks.

"And no leads, goddammit," he muttered.

The old man at the next table turned and stared at him. Roy made a dismissive gesture with one hand. "Don't mind me." He sent an apologetic smile across the air between them, and the man with the wool cap and lined face returned his attention to a newspaper and his dinner. If Roy was any judge, the man was a regular. Probably a widower who had most of his meals at this café, which meant he lived nearby.

A clock perched crookedly over the pass-through into the kitchen read a few minutes before nine at night. To fill the time before his dinner showed up, Roy pulled an iPad from his briefcase and let it find the cellular signal. He studied his map program, pinpointing his location with the built in GPS. He was north of Minneapolis, not far from the small farming community of Hinckley, but no one was farming in the middle of December. It was butt-ass cold outside, and snow lay on the ground in drifts and piles. A brisk wind blew south from the Arctic Circle. It was what had driven Roy inside.

"'Scuse me, hon." His overweight waitress dropped a plate overflowing with a steak, baked potato, and canned green beans, judging from their olive color, in front of him. "Want a refill on that coffee, hon?"

"Sure." Roy smiled at her. "That would be nice. What time do you close?"

She snorted. Makeup stuck in the lines in her face, lending her a garish aspect. Bleached blonde hair was pulled into a messy ponytail, and her blue eyes held a weary cast. "We don't, mister. Take your time."

He dug into his meal, realizing he hadn't eaten since the coffee and sweet roll he'd picked up at another nameless café for breakfast. The old man near him heaved a sigh and pushed to his feet. After a long pause, he stumbled toward the door. He might've walked better with a cane, but maybe pride forced him to do without.

Pride or money. Roy rolled his eyes and kept eating. He'd always been a loner, but it was pretty bad when he started attributing motives to total strangers he'd never see again. Keeping his eyes open and absorbing every single thing around him was hardwired in at this point. He'd done it for too long to stop.

He glanced at the map, wondering if it were wise to continue his current course of action, which was visiting the places each scientist had come from prior to signing on for the government's lab program. In two weeks, he'd blown a third of the way across the country, stopping at ten out-of-the-way towns, and come up with exactly nothing. He'd found a relative or two, but no one was willing to talk with him.

His next stop was Duluth, northeast of his current location. It wasn't far, but he'd had to make a pit stop. Peering through blowing snow exhausted him, and he worried he'd fall asleep at the wheel. Coffee and food had a salutary effect, though. He polished the rest of his potato and picked at the green beans. They tasted like all canned vegetables—terrible.

"Dessert, hon?" The waitress sidled back over to him, and Roy realized he was her only customer.

"Sure. What do you have?"

She rattled off a series of pies and cakes. He chose apple pie with a scoop of ice cream, and she left with his dinner plate. Roy slumped against the chair. He had to keep going. No choice. Not really. A good night's sleep, coupled with the first adequate meal he'd had in a couple days might make a big difference in his attitude. At least he hoped they would.

He'd just begun on the pie, which had a surprisingly flaky crust, when a rush of cold air yanked his attention toward the door. A tall woman walked in. Long, dark hair caked with snow swirled around her, and she held her body tightly as if she were really cold. Roy glanced at her feet and was shocked to see a pair of tennis shoes with holes in them. Good God, had she been outside with such inadequate footwear? Didn't she understand she could freeze to death? Even his stout boots didn't do much to divert the cold.

Keeping her gaze downcast, she made her way to the counter and sat.

"Coffee, hon?" The waitress asked.

"How much is it?" the woman inquired.

"Two bucks."

"Oh." The woman's shoulders drooped, and she swiveled the stool around, getting ready to go back out into the storm.

"No, you don't." The waitress's voice sharpened. "I'll stand you a coffee. You look about done in."

The woman's even features melted into what looked like relief before she turned back to face the counter. "Thank you. That's really kind and I appreciate it. My wallet was stolen, and—"

"Never you mind." The waitress patted the woman's shoulder. "Bet you're hungry too." She poured hot coffee into a mug and handed it to the woman, who drew the steaming liquid to her lips.

"Maybe a little," the woman ventured. She clasped the cup with fingers white from cold.

By now, Roy knew he was staring, but he couldn't make himself turn away. There was something waiflike and alluring about the tall woman with long, black hair. Snow dripped off her, creating puddles around her stool. All she wore against the winter weather was a thick, gray sweater and worn jeans. No scarf. No gloves. No hat. He was close to certain her wallet hadn't been stolen. She looked more like an abuse victim on the run to him. Maybe he could help her get to her intended destination, if it wasn't too far out of his way.

He pushed his chair back and made his way to the counter. "Say —" he began, but she started and drew away as if she expected him to hit her.

I was right. Abuse victim for sure.

"I'm not going to hurt you." He kept his voice low, soothing. "Order whatever you want, and I'll pay for it."

She kept her gaze on her hands clutching the coffee cup. "I can't let you do that, sir. I'm all right. Truly I am."

Without waiting for an invitation, he took the stool next to hers and called to the waitress. "Bring her the same meal I just had."

"You got it, hon," rang from the direction of the kitchen.

"You are not all right," Roy said. "You're thin as a rail, and you were shivering when you came in here. In fact, you still are. I'll bet your shoes are wet clear through." When she didn't respond, he ploughed on. "Let me help you."

She shook her head. "Don't want your kind of help. It always comes with strings."

"Mine doesn't."

He pushed a little with his enhanced mental ability to get her to look at him. If she did, maybe she'd see truth in his eyes. A shudder ran down her thin frame, but she dragged her gaze upward reluctantly. Roy felt bad for forcing her, but he didn't have time to soothe her wounded places, which he suspected ran deep.

Eyes a shade of green he'd never seen inspected him. Long, thick lashes framed those eyes, and they were set in a face with high cheekbones, a high forehead, and black eyebrows winging a track over porcelain skin.

"Who are you?" The words tore from him. He hadn't meant to say them. She was nervous as a feral cat as it was.

She shook her head sadly. "No one. I'm no one. You'll forget all about me when you leave here."

Something shifted in his mind, but he fought it. Before he could determine if something real had just happened or if he were imagining things, the waitress showed up with the woman's dinner.

"Here you go, hon. Hope medium's okay for that steak?"

"Fine, thank you." Before the words were out, the woman picked up the fork and knife and shoveled food into her mouth.

Roy congratulated himself on a good call. Even though she'd

been reluctant to admit it, she really was starving. He had no idea what she'd do tomorrow or the next day, but it wasn't his problem. While she ate, he observed her from the corner of his eyes. In addition to being hungry and underdressed, she looked young. Maybe twenty. He'd be surprised if she were much more than that.

He shook a mental finger at himself. The country was full of abused women running from the men who used them as punching bags before they raped them. It was one part of law enforcement work he'd never understood: why the women kept going back for more.

"There are safe houses for girls like you," he said, and could've kicked himself. What the hell was wrong with his mouth tonight? He couldn't seem to keep words on the other side of it.

She stopped chewing long enough to glance at him. "What's a safe house?"

"A place where women like you can go so whoever's after you can't get to you."

"What makes you think someone's after me?" Color splotched across her white cheeks.

Roy took a deep breath. "I was a cop for a long time."

Her entire body tightened, and he wondered if he'd been wrong about why she was out in the storm. "You said was." She swiped a paper napkin over her lips. "Are you still?"

"No. Not anymore."

She took another bite, clearly thinking about what he'd said. "These people you think are after me. Could they still find me in a safe house?"

He wanted to lie to her, but didn't. "Sure. Anyone can find anybody with the Internet and all, but the people who run the safe houses won't let anyone who might hurt you inside."

She drew her arched brows together and drank some coffee. "I'd have to go outside sometime. Work. Earn my way."

He nodded. Those things were all true. He scratched his head and pushed too-long hair out of his eyes. "Sometimes, when a man is really persistent, there are ways of setting you up with a different identity in a different part of the country."

Interest lit her features, and she cut up the last of her steak. "Where would I go to have that happen?"

"I'm not sure, but we could check with local agencies in the morning."

A blank expression washed over her face, as if someone had shut out a light. She shot him a look she might have given yesterday's overripe trash. "Morning, huh? You're just like all the rest of them, mister. Means I'd have to spend the night with you."

Roy winced. He hadn't been thinking. Of course she'd make that connection. "No." He shook his head emphatically. "I'd buy you your own room for the night. You can clean up, get some sleep, and we'll regroup in the morning after breakfast."

She narrowed her eyes, and he felt himself drawn into their depths. "My own room with a locked door?"

He nodded solemnly, willing her to believe him. If he could just do one decent deed, it would make up for the last two weeks of beating his head into a brick wall. Maybe it would give him enough juice to keep hunting for the scientists who were a bunch of Houdini fuckers.

"Mmph." She started on her potato, taking large bites. In between them, she said. "I'm trying to figure out your angle. If I've worked my way around to believing you won't hurt me by the time I'm done eating, I'll accept your offer."

It was the best he was likely to get. Roy stood. "Fair enough. I'm going to finish my pie." It was sitting in a pool of melted ice cream, but he didn't mind. "If you'd care to accept my help, just stop by my table on your way out. If you walk past, I give you my word I won't bother you."

"Deal." She said around a mouthful of food. Swallowing, she twisted to look at him.

It felt as if she were staring straight through him, but Roy held his ground even after he identified a zing of power withdrawing from his mind. What the hell was she, anyway? When she returned to her dinner, he retreated to his pie, thoughts racing a mile a minute. What the fuck was he doing? If he were smart, he'd forget his offer, throw enough money on the table to cover both meals, and run like hell for his car.

There was something about the woman, though, an appeal that drew him, snared him, and wouldn't leave him be. He ate mindlessly, not tasting the pie. He knew the feel of freak mind control. Was that it? Had he inadvertently stumbled onto one of *them?*

Impossible. They're never by themselves, and whatever she examined me with didn't feel quite right.

Plus, she didn't resemble the ones he'd killed before. They had dark hair, but animal eyes. Amber, not green like hers. Of course they'd been men, but simple genetics argued they'd all look much the same if they came out of the same petri dishes.

Were there other augmented humans beyond those he already knew about? The thought fascinated and chilled him at the same time.

He scraped his fork over the plate and realized it was empty. Slugging back long-since-cold coffee, he dug for his wallet and extracted what he was certain would cover dinner, laying bills on the table and placing his empty mug atop them.

The woman looked almost done with her meal. What would she do?

What would he do if she walked by him and out the door? Would he be able to keep his promise and not go after her?

CHAPTER 5

*G*lory stretched out the last of her meal to buy some thinking time. It had been a rough twelve days since she'd run from the compound. The first ride had taken her as far east as Spokane. He'd been nice, like she imagined a daddy or grandpa might be. The men after him less so. She'd had one narrow escape, but she'd only stunned him with her mental weaponry afraid if she left a trail of dead bodies, the entire world would hunt her down. She'd also been sparing about using her innate ability to shift reality. If too many odd things happened and people compared notes, it was only a matter of time before they identified her as the common denominator.

She'd sensed Nameless Ones the first few days, but managed to evade them by sending out chaff—electronic noise to mask her location. She needed things, money for one. Better clothing. Food. Everything had been a struggle. Her sheltered existence had proven far more of a handicap than she imagined it would. When it got down to it, she knew next to nothing about how to live on her own.

Even though she'd tried to hitch rides going south where it wasn't so cold, she ended up moving steadily east. Maybe it was better this way. If she could come up with winter clothing, it would be easier to lose herself in blizzard country. Even though she hadn't sensed them lately, the Nameless Ones hadn't given up.

Glory wasn't under any illusions; they'd hunt her forever.

Her last ride, a long haul trucker, left her off a few miles down the road. Booted her out of his rig, actually, once he figured out she wasn't kidding when she refused to fuck him, suck him off, or fondle him. His parting shot, through teeth stained from chewing tobacco, had been he hoped she froze to death.

And I damn near did before I saw the lights for this place.

Glory gave herself a mental shake. She had to make a choice. Was the man watching her from the table what he appeared? She'd risked a scan of his mind, not going very deep, but deep enough to see things she didn't like. He hunted those like her. She'd plucked images of Nameless Ones from his visual cortex and sensed the man's shock and confusion as she withdrew from his mind. At least so far, though, he didn't identify her as prey. Maybe for a few hours, at least until he helped her find one of the safe houses he'd talked about, she could continue to fool him.

Snow battered the café's windows and wind howled around the building. She had to leave here sometime. What were the odds of getting another ride in the midst of this storm? She'd hoped the last trucker would agree to hide her as he crossed over into Canada, and he might have if she'd been more cooperative.

Another mental shake. Her mind was wandering.

Glory set her fork down and swiveled her chair to stand. The man was looking right at her, but he dropped his gaze. "It's okay." She walked to where he sat. "I've decided to accept your offer."

When he looked at her, relief lightened his features, and shockingly blue eyes crinkled at the edges as he smiled. He had a square jaw, defined cheekbones, and a high forehead. Unkempt black hair fell to his collarbones. A hint of red brown roots suggested he dyed his hair, but why? Did men even do things like that?

He stood, and she looked at him, really looked and saw a man somewhere north of his middle-thirties. He was taller than her by a couple inches with impossibly broad shoulders. A stretchy dark blue top outlined slabs of muscle running along his shoulders and down his arms. Faded black trousers hung low on his slim hips, and a flat stomach disappeared beneath his waistband. He plucked a thick jacket from his chair, zipped into it, and followed it with a storm parka that sported a fur-lined hood.

"I'm Roy Kincaid." He held out a hand.

"Glory." She shook briefly, using the touch to try to see a little more of who he was.

"Do you have a last name, Glory?"

No one else had asked. "Robertson," she blurted, and hoped to hell she sounded convincing. If he'd been a cop, he had to have experience reading peoples' lies.

He shot an odd look her way, and she knew she'd been busted. "It's okay, Glory," he said. "Maybe by morning you'll feel safe enough to tell me. The folks who run the safe house will need to know."

He glanced at a window next to the front door and shrugged out of his storm parka. "Here." He draped it around her shoulders. "Put it on at least until we're inside the car. I don't really need it. This jacket I have on is plenty thick and warm."

Glory didn't argue. The garment was warm from his body, and it smelled like him, spicy and masculine. For the first time in her life, she wondered what a man's arms would feel like around her if she wasn't struggling to escape. He popped an electronic tablet into a black leather briefcase and zipped it up before jerking his chin toward the door.

"Ready?"

She nodded and followed him. He held the door against the wind, and she pushed her way outside. Pins and needles shot through her feet as cold assaulted them. He'd been right about her shoes being soaked. Maybe by morning they'd be dry. She waited for him to lead the way to a beat-up Toyota 4Runner. He hit an electronic device, and the car chirped and lit up inside. Maybe its external appearance was deceptive. She knew, from shows she'd picked up over the Internet, undercover cops often drove inconspicuous cars.

All he said was he used to be a cop. I have no idea if he worked undercover or not. Plus, I have no clue what he does right now.

"Get in." He opened her door and scooped something off the floor from the passenger footwall.

Glory cringed backward, unsure of her choice to go with him. "What's that?"

"Calm down. It's a brush to get snow off the windows."

Heat flooded her face, a counterpart to stinging cold, and she slid into the passenger seat, feeling like an idiot. He tossed a set of keys into her lap. "Start the car, would you? It'll get the defroster heating faster."

He shut the door to keep the storm out, and she picked up the bundle of keys. There were so many of them, how would she ever figure out which one to use?

Never mind. I can do this.

She peered at each key. Located one with a sigil that matched the sigil on the steering column and punched the key into the ignition, twisting it until an unpleasant high-pitched whine made her back off. The engine hummed along, though, so she figured she'd done okay.

Roy pulled open the driver's door and slapped the long-handled brush against it. Once it was clean, he got into the car, kicking snow off his boots against the rocker panel. Wind bellowed around the car like a live thing trying to get at them, and Glory wrapped her arms around herself, glad for the added weight and warmth of Roy's parka.

He slammed his door and turned to her. "No one ever taught you to drive, did they?"

The heat that had suffused her face earlier returned in spades. "That obvious, huh?"

"You ground the starter motor." He paused a beat. "It's all right. You didn't hurt anything. Toyota builds these babies tough. They can take a lot of abuse."

"Where are we going?" Glory wanted to move the subject away from her lack of driving skills.

He fiddled with a lighted display on the dashboard, and a map flared to life. "Not very far in this storm." He traced a line on the map with his index finger. "We're on the northern outskirts of Hinckley. Hopefully, we'll find a motel once we get to the next town. If not, we'll just keep looking. Duluth's not all that far, and there are sure to be lots of choices once we get closer."

Glory gazed at the display. "Does the computer have a weather channel?" she asked.

"It's not exactly a computer, but yes it does. Not sure we need one. This storm's predicted to last through tomorrow night."

"That long." She bit her lip. She'd have to watch her questions since they exposed her ignorance of things most people probably knew about.

"You're not from around here, are you?" He slipped the car into gear, and they nosed through drifts and out onto the roadway.

"Why would you ask?" she countered.

"For one thing, your speech pattern. You don't talk like you're from Minnesota, or the Midwest for that fact."

Something else she'd never considered. How she talked might be a dead giveaway. She framed her next question carefully. "Where do you think I'm from?"

"West coast." He waited. When she didn't say anything, he pressed, "Am I right?"

"Uh-huh." Her heart picked up speed, and she rustled through her database of a brain. It was too late with Roy, but she'd have to cultivate different speech patterns to enhance the odds of remaining hidden.

"See," he went on. "Listen to how I talk. It's subtle, but my vowels are longer, and the inflection's slightly different for many of my words. For someone who's attuned to listening, it would let them know I'm from the East Coast, but haven't lived there consistently."

Now that he pointed it out, she had noticed, but hadn't paid it much mind. It would take far more than she'd anticipated to blend into this world so she was close to invisible.

I can do this. I just need a couple breaks.

The Toyota crawled down the highway at a snail's pace. She supposed they couldn't go any faster because it was hard to see where the road was. Something flashed across her vision through the driving snow. At first she wondered if she'd imagined it, if her visual center was malfunctioning because she was so tired, but Roy banged a fist on the steering wheel.

"Fuck!" He shook his head. "Sorry, Glory. I'll try to watch my language."

"What's wrong?" The lights flickered again, more strongly this time.

"There's a roadblock up ahead. They must be monitoring the road because of the storm."

Sudden fear closed around her heart like a fist and squeezed hard. "If they're going to stop us anyway, let's turn around now."

He reached across the divider and laid a hand on her upper arm. "It's the Minnesota Highway Patrol, not your husband or boyfriend. Get hold of yourself."

What if you're wrong?

"But we have to turn around anyway," she persisted.

"Probably. Let's see what they have to say. Plus, they'll know where the closest lodging is."

It sounded reasonable, but something made the back of her neck prickle uncomfortably. "You probably already think I'm a little nuts," she forced a small laugh, "but would you mind if I crawled into the back seat and pretended to be asleep?"

He patted her shoulder. "If that'll make you feel better, Glory, I don't mind at all."

~

ROY NOSED the 4Runner to a halt at the roadblock. As he expected, two Highway Patrol cars were pulled at right angles across the road. He activated the electric window and fumbled for his CIA creds, which he flashed at the officer who lumbered to his open window.

The big man's tired brown eyes widened. "Agent Kincaid. What brings you to our neck of the woods on a night like this?"

Roy shot him a *you should know better than to ask* look. "Can't tell you that, Sergeant."

"I suppose I can let you through, since you've probably had all them fancy defensive driving classes," the sergeant muttered.

"I'd consider it a kindness," Roy said. "I have appointments in Duluth in the morning." He shot an engaging smile at the cop.

"Just take her slow," the man cautioned. "We're supposed to get another foot and a half before this storm blows herself out. Plows can't keep up with it."

"Any motels between here and Duluth?"

"Lots of 'em, but they're probably mostly shut up for the night on account of the storm. Keep your eyes open for neon, though. You just never know."

"Thanks." Roy reached for the button to shut his window, but saw another officer making his way to the Toyota and waited to see what the man wanted.

"Never mind, Jeb." The sergeant waved his partner back. "This here's a spook."

"Well, we're supposed to ask everyone," the second man insisted. He was shorter and not as burly as the sergeant.

"Ask everyone what?" Roy quirked a brow. Cold wind blew through the car, whitening his knuckles where they rested on the steering wheel.

The second officer pulled a photograph from an inside pocket and shoved it and a penlight through the window. Roy played the light over the photograph and was grateful for all the years he'd played poker. He handed both back. "Who exactly is she?" He kept his voice even, devoid of inflection.

"We're not rightly sure." The officer sounded uncomfortable. "The APB didn't list a name, which seemed odd to me, but she escaped from a mental institution in California, and her folks are worried sick about her. They've activated a nationwide alert. Next time you turn on a television, you'll probably hear more about it."

"I'll be sure to keep my eyes open." Roy looked from one man to the other. "Is that all?"

"Sure, Agent Kincaid. You're free to go." The sergeant moved back to the shelter of his vehicle with his partner close behind.

Roy rolled up his window and wove around the two Highway Patrol cars, his mind racing. He was pretty good at spotting mental illness, and Glory certainly didn't fit the bill. Whoever she was running from had resources. Enough to manipulate national media into helping them.

"Thank you."

Her voice from the backseat startled him. "Who are you running from?" he asked, aiming for a non-threatening tone. "You have to tell me. If they're powerful enough to get your picture on the television networks, maybe a safe house isn't such a good idea."

When she didn't reply, he hurried on. "You must have heard that I work for the CIA. We have ways of hiding people, but you've got to give me something to work with, Glory. I can't help you if you keep me in the dark."

"When we get to Duluth, just let me go. I'll figure this out."

He blew out a tight breath. "You don't get it. If your face is all over network news and the Internet, someone is bound to recognize you. How long have you been on the run?"

"Twelve days. No, maybe thirteen." Rustling from the back seat and a glance in his mirror told him she'd sat up.

Roy nodded to himself. The timing was about right for whoever was after her to decide they needed help. After the first forty-eight hours, trails did nothing but get progressively colder.

"I can't force you to trust me," he said, "but right now, I'm your best bet. I'm guessing you don't have any money. You're in snow country, and you need a crash course in altering your appearance. We need to bleach your hair, cut it short, and cover up those eyes. They're a dead giveaway."

"I have contacts—"

"Then for Christ's sake take them out," he cut in.

"No, it's the other way round. I have contacts to make my eyes look brown, but after a while they hurt, so I took them out. They're hard lenses. The soft ones don't cover color as well. Anyway, I wrapped them in a tissue and found a plastic container so I wouldn't lose them."

Definitely not from a mental hospital. Not if someone made certain she had contact lenses to obscure her eyes.

When he caught a peek in the rearview mirror, she'd buried her head in her hands. Roy's heart squeezed painfully in his chest. What had happened to her? He fought an urge to pull the car to a halt, move into the back seat, and fold her into his arms. He might have if there'd been any safe spot, but drifts lined both sides of the road.

"I won't hurt you, Glory. I promise." Roy winced. What if he couldn't keep that promise? What if—? He shut his thoughts down.

A muted sob skimmed against his ears, followed by another. He didn't know what else to say, so he drove in silence, his thoughts a jumble, while the enigma in the backseat cried as if her heart were breaking.

Roy tried to make sense of what little he knew. She'd stumbled over a last name, didn't know how to drive, had no money, and he'd bet his last buck she had no identification. He pulled his cell phone out of a pocket and texted HQ on their secure line, asking for a list of cults in the U.S. and Europe with strong financial backing. The car swerved on the icy road, but he was done with his phone and dropped it into one of the pigeonholes in the center divider.

"Did you just turn me in?" Her voice was thick with tears.

"No, Glory. I'm trying to figure things out. You won't answer my questions, so I'm asking someone else."

"Who else knows about me?" Her voice developed shrill overtones.

He activated the childproof locking mechanism in case she was contemplating throwing herself out one of the back doors. "Hush. Settle down. When you're feeling better, come on back up here, and we can talk."

CHAPTER 6

*G*lory bit down on a finger to force a return of rational thought. She had to stop crying, had to think. There must be a way out of this. Like Roy had suggested, she could alter her appearance so at least she wouldn't be a dead ringer at first glance. The Nameless Ones had done the unthinkable. Somehow, they'd corralled humans into instigating a search for her.

Escapee from a mental hospital. What a perfect story. That way, no one would believe her. They'd chalk up whatever she said to the delusions of a deranged woman. It also meant she was cut off from doing anything that might draw attention. No more pushing into people's minds, no more hurting them, and definitely no more twisting events to meet her needs. Not that she'd done very much of any of those things, but she had to quit immediately—even if her life was on the line.

What about Roy? At least she knew a little more about him. She was shocked the CIA targeted the Nameless Ones. Was it because of things like the data heist she pulled?

Hell, I have no idea what I gathered from that computer. Should've looked.

Right. No time, plus the Nameless Ones would have skinned me alive if they found out.

She scrubbed her hands down her face and worked her way back over the divider and into the front seat, snatching up his phone as she did so. He was watching, but didn't say anything when she tapped the text icon and read what he'd sent.

"Tell them not to waste their time," she said as she put the phone back where she'd gotten it. "I'm not from a cult, not one anyone knows about, anyway."

"This non-cult, does it have a name?"

She shook her head. "I've read about cults. They're like those deals in Utah with plural wives, or the fanatics who all kill themselves when things go wrong."

"Both of those fit the bill," he agreed, "but there are lots of kinds of cults. Most have religious overtones of some kind, but not all of them."

"Tell me about you." She shifted topics, scared if she said much more she'd inadvertently give something away.

"Not much to tell. I started working for the CIA right out of law school when I was twenty-five. Why? What difference do I make?"

She sent a glance skittering his way. "I'm still trying to decide if I can trust you. Why'd you tell me you used to be a cop if you've had the same job all along?"

The line of his jaw tightened. "I avoid disclosing what I do in public places, but you'd asked me a question, so I gave you a plausible answer. It was the truth. CIA agents are glorified cops with a whole lot more training. You looked so terrified, I was afraid if I said I was still a cop, you'd bolt."

"Mmph. Doesn't exactly make it easier to trust you."

"Some days I don't even trust me." He drew a breath and blew it out. "If I had bad intentions, I'd have turned you in to the cops back at the roadblock. Or if I had the other kind of bad intentions, I'd have turned off on a side road. There haven't been many, but a few. I'm much stronger than you, and it wouldn't be hard to—"

"Stop!" She held up a hand. "I don't even like talking about things like that." She pressed her lips together to keep them from trembling. "Your intentions seem aboveboard—at least so far."

"What the hell happened to you?" He shook his head. "Sorry. That came out harsh, and I didn't mean it to. Christ! You can't be much past twenty. How old are you, anyway? Where are your parents? Who did such a shit job raising you that you flinch every time I look at you?"

"I— I can't answer any of those things."

"You can't even divulge how old you are?" he sputtered.

"I don't know. Not precisely. Somewhere between nineteen and twenty-two, but I can't tack it down any better than that."

"Why not?"

Glory pressed her tongue against her teeth. She'd almost told him because she could only remember the last seven years, but talking would only get her into trouble with this man. He had a sharp, analytical mind and giving him data would just lead to more questions. Lights rose out of the gloom, and Roy skidded into the right hand lane. She balled her hands into fists in her lap. Was this where he'd get off the highway and order her out of his car like the trucker had?

After he asked for his coat back.

She girded herself for the worst. At least there were clusters of lights, which meant people. Maybe someone would— And then she remembered what the highway patrol said about her face being plastered all over the media. She couldn't ask anyone for help. Wouldn't put them in the difficult position of deciding whether to shield her or turn her in. No. She was on her own.

The car rolled to a stop, and she glanced out the front window. To spare Roy the difficulty of telling her this was it, she squared her shoulders and reached for the door latch. "Thanks for everything," she murmured. "I'll be on my way now." She shrugged out of his heavy parka and laid it between them.

He closed his hand around her upper arm. "The hell."

"Stop." She tried to pull away, but she may as well have been tethered to a boulder. "You're hurting me."

"You're not thinking straight." He grabbed her chin with his other hand and twisted her head to face him. "I stopped here to go shopping for you. We're at Wal-mart."

"But it's nighttime."

"They stay open late. Some are open 24/7. You need winter clothes and hair dye and boots. What sizes do you wear?"

She jerked her chin out of his grasp and stared at the floorboards. "You stopped here to get things for me?" It was a simple concept. Why was she having such a hard time with it?

Maybe because no one's ever done anything nice for me before—ever.

"Yes." Roy lowered his voice, which had gotten louder. "Sizes?"

She chewed her lower lip. "I don't know," she finally admitted.

He let go of her arm. "I can do a pretty good job guessing except for shoes. Give me one of yours."

She reached down and pulled the sodden tennis shoe off her right foot, handing it to him. He punched a button, and a light went on above her. He held the shoe beneath it, twisting it this way and that before handing it back to her and turning the light out.

"I'm going to leave the engine running so you don't get cold."

"Wouldn't it be easier if I went inside with you?" She pulled his coat back around her.

"Of course it would, but you can't. Once we've cut and bleached your hair, you'll have a little more latitude." He dropped the cell phone into a pocket and got out of the car, shutting the door behind him.

Glory sat in the darkened vehicle, enjoying the blast of warm air from the heater bathing her feet. Time dripped by. Fifteen minutes, then half an hour. She fiddled with the satellite radio and listened to music, before tuning to an Oprah talk show. Why was Roy doing all this for her? What would he want in return? No one was this decent...

"I don't know that." She spoke aloud to soothe herself. "When you get down to it, I don't know much of anything, except how to mollify the Nameless Ones and live in the compound." A thought slammed into her, and she tucked her legs beneath her butt on the seat. Roy hunted Nameless Ones. She'd seen it in his mind. She hated them too. Maybe that meant they were on the same side.

Maybe not. Depends on why he's hunting them.

She tried to figure out a way to ask him about what he did, but he probably wouldn't tell her. She couldn't reveal what she'd discovered snooping in his mind. She also couldn't disclose any of her other special talents.

Even if I told him, he'd never believe me. Maybe then, he'd buy that cock-and-bull story about me being from a mental hospital.

Glory smiled in spite of herself. She was beginning to like Roy. To trust him. That was dangerous ground. Maybe she should run while she could and leave him out of the mess she'd made of things.

The Nameless Ones would kill him if he stood between them and her. She clawed at her throat, suddenly unable to breathe. Roy would protect her. Even though she didn't know much about how the world worked, she felt certain he'd pit himself between her and her Handlers. Panic swelled through every nerve ending, and she fumbled with the door latch.

Got to get out of here.

Can't stay.

Roy will be in danger.

But the door didn't open. She wriggled across the console to the driver's seat and tried that door. It was locked too. She remembered the light switch, flicked it on, and studied the buttons on the driver's door. Finding one that looked promising, she pressed it and heard the automatic locks disengage.

Glory turned the dome light and radio off and opened the car door. Cold air hit her like a wall, displacing air from her lungs. She had no idea it got this cold anywhere in the world. Her nose and throat ached with it and her hands numbed, along with her toes. She stood and picked a direction. One was as good as any other.

She'd be dead within an hour or two in these temperatures. She sent one longing glance back inside the warm car before she pushed the door shut and started walking. She hadn't been able to force herself to give up Roy's parka and hoped he'd forgive her for stealing from him.

Heavy footsteps pounded toward her, and then Roy swept her into his arms and held her tight against his body. "I was afraid you'd do something stupid," he muttered, his words nearly lost in the wind buffeting them.

"Not stupid." She butted her head back so she could talk. "You're in danger if I stay. I have to—"

He laid a gloved hand over her mouth. "Danger is where I live. Please, get back in the car. I left the shopping cart once I saw what you were doing. I need to go get it." He let go of her and pulled the car door open, guiding her through it.

She slid back inside, shivering uncontrollably. The back door opened, and Roy tossed bags into the car—lots of them. She couldn't believe all that could possibly be for her. He settled into the driver's seat and turned to face her. "At least you were smart enough to keep my coat. We can sort everything out once we find a motel."

"You should've let me go," she said through chattering teeth.

"Did you think I wouldn't be able to track you?"

"Huh?"

"Your footprints in the snow. They'd have led away from this car. Jesus! It's minus fifty degrees outside, and that's without factoring in the wind-chill. You'd have been dead in a couple hours. It's gotten colder since you came into that diner near Hinckley."

Unfamiliar feelings buffeted her. Even though leaving was the right thing to do, she was relieved and grateful Roy had stopped her. So far tonight, she'd experienced sharp tides of feeling. She'd cried because her heart ached, not because she'd been beaten and her body hurt. The Nameless Ones had told her again and again she was one scant step up from an animal. Had they been wrong?

~

ROY SLIPPED the transmission into low and made his way out of the parking lot. Rather than getting back on the highway, he turned left and made his way down a frontage road. Where there were Wal-Marts, there were always motels. Neon flickered through driving snow, and he turned in when he saw a vacancy sign.

"Be right back," he said. "I'll get us rooms next to each other. Hopefully with adjoining doors, so I can help with your hair."

Before she could protest, he was gone. He smiled to himself as he strode into the badly lit office. Glory had been about to say she could do her own hair, but it was pure bluff. She didn't have the first idea of how to do anything but wash it and brush it out, which might explain why it was so long.

The smell of curry assaulted Roy's nostrils. An older East Indian man, complete with a turban, got up from a chair and stood behind the counter. "Help you, sir?"

Roy nodded. "Two rooms, next to each other, for my sister and me."

"I can do that, sir. Smoking or not?"

"Not."

Roy paid with cash and was back outside with two keys in under five minutes. He drove them around to the backside of the motel and handed Glory one of the keys. "Open the door. I'll be right behind you."

"Let me carry something." She got out of the car and pulled the back door open, grabbing a couple shopping bags. Balancing them under one arm, she jockeyed the door open with the other and walked into her room.

Roy dropped the bags he was carrying on the scarred table and went back for another load. Once he'd gotten the last of his purchases, he shut the door, twisted the deadbolt, and slipped a chain affair into a socket. "Do you see what I did?" he asked.

"Yes. Two locks and a chain."

"When I leave, you lock up the same way."

"Okay."

"Look through what I bought," he said. "I may have forgotten a thing or two. See that door?" He pointed at a door along the inside wall. When she nodded, he went on. "I'll take my things into the next room and give you a few minutes. We should take care of your hair tonight. I'll tap on the door and you can let me in. Leave the outer door locked no matter what."

Leaving her with a shell-shocked expression—maybe he'd sounded too much like a CIA operative—Roy moved his briefcase and a duffel bag into his room. He locked the car, retreated to his room, and set the heat on high. That done, he fired up his iPad and checked to see what The Company had sent about cults. The list was long, and he studied its high points before retrieving a pair of scissors from his duffel and knocking on the adjoining door.

Glory opened it almost instantaneously, which pleased him. She might have gone the other route and told him she'd see him in the morning. Worse, she might have left, though he didn't think she'd try that again. Although now that she had adequate winter clothing, she might reconsider fleeing.

Roy brandished the shears and motioned her to a chair, but she backed away with even more of a deer-in-the-headlights look than she'd had before. "What? They're only scissors."

She pointed to his side holster and the 9mm Sig Sauer tucked in its worn leather folds. "You didn't have that in the café."

"Oh yes I did. It was in my briefcase." Roy set the scissors on the table and extended his hands palms up. "This is what I do. Who I am. I've carried a gun so long, it's second nature; plus you're safer this way."

She clamped her jaws together so hard he heard her teeth clack against each other. "Sorry. It was just a shock seeing it." She tilted her chin at a defiant angle. "Let's get my makeover online so we can both get some sleep."

Roy blew out the breath he'd been holding, grateful she wasn't going to perseverate about the gun. And then he thought about hair and DNA and leaving evidence. He couldn't very well cut her hair outside. "Wait a minute," he told her.

"Why? What do we need?"

"I'm going out to the car for newspapers. We'll spread them under that chair and when we're done, I can fold them up. That way, we won't leave any of your hair laying around. While I'm gone, why not put on one of the long sleeved stretchy shirts I bought?"

She didn't say anything, so he left her room and got what he needed.

The newspapers were a good call. She had a lot of hair. When he was done, it piled around their feet. Roy stood back and inspected his work, snipping a few more strands here and there. The short do hugged her jawline and opened the upper lines of her body. Broad shoulders were much more obvious without her long hair. Bands of muscle ran across them and circled both arms.

He waved her out of the chair and gathered up the newspapers. "Do you work out?"

"Of course. Every day in the arena." She clapped a hand over her mouth, and he knew she hadn't meant to disclose quite so much.

"Did you find the hair color?" he asked. At her nod, he said, "Let me dump the hair in their incinerator. It'll take me a little to get a fire going in this weather then I'll come back, and we can finish up."

"Do you want me to lock the door behind you?"

Roy smiled. "Fast learner. Yes, I'll knock twice and you let me in."

HE DUCKED BACK inside her room and locked the door, shaking snow off his boots and jacket. After draping the jacket on a wall hook, he glanced at Glory. She'd moved to the same chair where he'd cut her hair and sat motionless, holding the box of hair color between her hands. "I read the instructions," she said, her voice devoid of any emotion. "I think I can do this."

"Let me help you put it on," he said. "It's especially hard in the back where you can't see."

She narrowed her eyes. "You dye your hair, don't you?"

Roy took a step back. The question was so out of the blue, it caught him by surprise. He walked to a wall-mounted mirror and looked at himself with a critical eye. When he turned to Glory, he grinned sheepishly. "Caught me dead to rights."

"But why?" she asked. "Men, er most men don't…" Her voice ran down.

"I do a lot of night work. My natural color has a lot of red in it. Black blends in better."

Glory nodded, a solemn expression on her face. She thrust the Clairol box his way. "I'm ready, I guess."

He pulled the only other chair around to face her. She looked even younger and more vulnerable with her cropped hair. He leaned toward her and placed a hand on her knee. "Did you get a chance to look through the clothes I bought?"

She nodded and glanced away, her eyes suddenly shiny with tears. "Thank you. They're all wonderful."

"Do they fit? How about the boots?"

"Maybe a little bit big, but you got thick socks, and they'll be perfect with them."

He tightened his hand on her knee. "Why are you crying?"

"It doesn't matter." She focused her gaze on him, and he noticed the green in her eyes shaded from darker to lighter as iris moved toward pupil. "Once we're done with my hair, and I've slept, I need to find my own way. I have clothes now, and I'll look different enough, I might be safe."

"No!" The word burst from Roy, surprising the crap out him, and he muttered, "Sorry, not quite sure—"

"It's for the best. The longer you stay with me, the higher the odds they'll find us."

Roy got up so fast his chair clattered to the floor. He covered the distance between them in less than a heartbeat and dragged her upright and into his arms. She stiffened, but then relaxed against him, and he closed his arms tightly around her.

"I don't understand this," he said, "but I want to keep you close, protect you. I felt that way the moment you walked into the diner."

"It's a mistake." Her words were muffled against his collarbone.

"Maybe so," he replied, "but it's my mistake." Leaning back slightly, he angled his head and closed his mouth gently over hers. It was an experimental kiss, one she could draw away from easily, except she didn't.

When Roy realized she was kissing him back, his heart soared, and the tight rein he held over his emotions shattered.

CHAPTER 7

Glory threaded her fingers into Roy's hair and pulled him into their kiss. Her gut squirmed uncomfortably. Part of her screamed what they were doing wasn't very smart, but the feel of Roy's arms around her and the rough press of his mouth on hers wakened something primitive in her, a part she had no idea existed. She wanted the man in her arms. Wanted to rip the clothes off his body and examine him with hands, and eyes, and mouth. She recognized arousal, but she'd never associated it with anything other than fantasies and her own hands.

He murmured wordless endearments against her mouth and brushed his lips over her forehead, cheeks, and eyebrows before returning to her mouth. He licked and nibbled her lips until she opened them, and he sank his tongue inside her mouth. The sensation sent shivers from her belly to her suddenly damp crotch, and she tightened her hold on him. Her nipples hardened where they pressed against his chest, and she sparred with his tongue, sucking on it.

His breathing quickened, and she felt his cock swell against her belly. He kneaded her back with strong hands and ran them downward where he cupped the curves of her ass for long moments before ripping his mouth from hers. He stumbled a few steps from her. "Sorry." His gaze was full of pain and longing. "I'm sorry. Shouldn't have done that."

Since she suspected she shouldn't have either, Glory turned away. Beyond the obvious faux pas of kissing him back in the first place, had she done something else wrong? Had he stopped because she didn't kiss well or because…?

She took a deep breath and forced words out. "I'm sorry too. It's the first time I've ever kissed a man—well, when I wanted to, that is. Guess I botched it."

He drew his brows together. "When you wanted to? Did whoever held you captive force you to have sex?" He balled his hands into fists. "If they did that, I'll track those motherfuckers until the moon falls out of the sky, and they'll be dog meat once I find them."

She swallowed half a smile. Who could have guessed how good it felt to have someone stick up for you? Glory shook her head. "No. I was off limits. The other girls too." She closed her teeth over her lower lip. Maybe she could tell him just a little. "One of my Handlers got out of control. I was trying to protect the other girls, so I agreed to go with him."

"Not sounding good." A muscle twitched in Roy's jaw. "Did that bastard rape you?"

"He would have, but no."

Roy made come along motions with two fingers. "Don't make me drag this out of you. How'd you get away? Granted you're tall for a woman. And you look pretty strong, but still you wouldn't be a match for most men."

Sweetheart, if you only knew.

"I, um, knocked him out and ran."

Roy crossed his arms over his chest. "Going to have to do better than that."

She straightened her spine. "Okay. I killed him and ran."

A surprised look flashed across Roy's rugged face, but it was gone almost instantly. He'd obviously trained himself to give little to nothing away. "What'd you use? Gun? Knife?"

She studied the motel's worn carpet. "Doesn't matter. Dead is dead."

"Have you killed before?" Curiosity underscored his words.

She shook her head. "Let's get going with my hair. I don't want to talk about this anymore."

"Killing in self-defense isn't a crime," he went on as if he hadn't heard her. "I know people who could help you—"

"I said I don't want to talk about it," she cut in, scared shitless he'd find out too much.

He nodded and made a grab for the Clairol box, pulling bottles and gloves out of it. He poured one bottle into the other, cut the tip off the applicator lid, and shook the contents gently. While he peeled plastic gloves off the instructions, he said, "Sit back in the chair, please. I bought you a comb and brush. Are they still in one of the bags?"

"No. I moved them into the bathroom. I'll get them."

She made a quick trip to the small bathroom. Once she'd handed the items over, she settled into the chair, shut her eyes, and let him work the bleach into her hair. From reading the directions, she knew it would take at least forty-five minutes to leach the darkness from her locks and more time for toner, but she wouldn't need him front and center once the bleach was in place.

Glory debated whether to ask the question batting around in her head, but the more she learned about being human, the easier it would be for her to blend in. She cleared her throat against the bleach fumes. "Before you got all fussed up about me being a rape victim, I asked if I'd botched kissing you."

"You must want to know, or you wouldn't have asked again." He placed the empty hair color bottle back in its box and went into the bathroom where she heard water running. When he returned, he'd taken the gloves off.

"Yes, I do want to know, and you still haven't told me." She winced. "Was I that bad?"

He hooked the other chair with his foot and dropped into it, so he sat facing her. "You were wonderful. Too wonderful." He laced his fingers together in his lap, squeezing until the knuckles turned white. "I had a wife once. We weren't married long. One of the organized crime groups kidnapped her. They were trying to force my hand, and it would have worked…" He swallowed, his throat working with emotion. "Except some asshole got trigger happy and killed her before I could deliver their demands."

Compassion flooded her, and she scooted her chair close enough to place a hand over where his knotted together in his lap. "I'm so sorry."

He sent a rueful smile skittering her way. "Not half as sorry as me. Lorna would still be alive if she hadn't fallen in love with me." Roy swallowed again. "It's been nine years, and I've kept to myself since then. I swore no one would ever lose their life again because of me."

She didn't know what to say, how to comfort him, so she squeezed his clasped hands, offering wordless support. "The work you do…" She took a breath and started over. "People must die sometimes with what you do. Otherwise you wouldn't carry a gun."

"They do. It's not easy when I lose men in my patrols—I always feel responsible, but they knew what they were getting into when they signed on."

Glory thought about that, and her next words were hesitant. "I don't really know very much—about anything, but Lorna must have realized your job had risks."

"Sure," he agreed, "but not necessarily to her."

Glory swiped at a dollop of bleach running down her forehead. "Still, you did everything you could."

"You're trying to make me feel better. Thanks for that." He glanced at his watch.

"How much more time?"

"At least twenty minutes."

She nibbled her lower lip. She didn't really want him to leave, but it would be best—for both of them. "You don't have to stay. I can take it from here."

He shook his head. "I just shared some pretty personal shit. Very few people know about Lorna." He made a snorting noise. "Lots of the other spooks are convinced I'm gay."

Glory understood. "You told me something, now you want quid pro quo." He nodded and raised his gaze to meet hers.

"It's safer if you don't know. Hell, you burned my hair after you cut it, and I'm guessing you're either going to burn the hair color bottles or take them with us." She narrowed her eyes. "You're being really careful, even though you have no idea what's after me."

"I'm always careful. It's why I'm still alive. In terms of not knowing who's after you, I'll take my chances." Fire flashed from his blue eyes. He'd said *danger is where I live*, and she didn't doubt his assessment for a moment.

She looked away. "It really is best if you go back to your own room. I read how to check to make sure all the black's out of my hair. I'll rinse the bleach, put the other stuff on for fifteen minutes, and then wash everything out."

Something shuttered in his face, as if a light had extinguished. Roy got stiffly to his feet and nodded. "If that's what you want."

"Maybe not what I want, but it's for the best," she repeated and stood. "Thanks, Roy. For everything. I'm not sure what I'd have done if you weren't in that café."

"You're welcome." His voice held a gruff note, and he walked through the adjoining door into his own room. The noise of the double doors shutting held a finality that told her exactly what she needed to do. She'd waffled before, been weak. Roy would stand by her; he was that kind of man. But she couldn't let him throw his life away. She hadn't said so, but their situation wasn't all that different than his had been with his wife.

A sad smile split her face, and she picked through the clothing he'd bought, arranging it in neat piles. He'd picked up a medium sized backpack too, so she had somewhere to stash what she wasn't wearing. She placed long underwear, heavy socks and layers of outerwear off to one side and folded everything else into the backpack. By the time she was done, it was time to check her hair.

ROY SAT to unlace his Arctic pac boots. Once they were loose, he toed them off. He grabbed the iPad and flopped onto the bed, never taking his gaze from the door leading into Glory's room. "What the fuck is wrong with me?" he muttered. Not that he hadn't had his share of no strings sex over the years, but he'd steered clear of women as soon as he started to feel anything beyond simple lust. He'd broken a cardinal rule with Glory by kissing a woman he felt something for.

Don't be ridiculous.

I just met her. How could I possibly feel anything at all?

To divert himself, he scrolled through email, caught up on news, and researched half a dozen cults from his requested search. She'd said not to bother, but he needed to do something. When she inferred she'd come close to being assaulted, his head had damn near exploded with the need to fight back.

Aside from cults, he ran every odd group he'd come across through his mind, but she didn't exactly fit the description for any of them. She was bright, quick to grasp things, despite saying she didn't know very much. He'd studied her body while they chatted, and he cut her hair. Quite aside from her obvious female assets—high, full breasts, a narrow waist, and flared hips—she was damn near perfectly proportioned, and she moved with a dancer's grace.

She'd mentioned training in an arena. Was that it? Had she been given martial arts training? Was that why she glided when she walked?

Roy pounded a fist on the bed. He needed answers, damn it, and he didn't have many more for her than for the scientists he sought. His cell vibrated in his pocket. When he glanced at the display, it read Private.

He punched the green Answer icon and barked, "Kincaid."

Silence rolled through the cellular lines for long enough he pulled the phone away from his ear and looked at the display to make certain the call was still connected. He softened his voice, but not his words. "This is Agent Kincaid. If you don't say something in the next ten seconds, I'm going to hang up."

"Sorry." A wavering masculine voice crackled over the phone's speaker.

Kincaid rolled his eyes. "You're running your voice through an amplitude modifier to scramble its pattern. Who are you, and what the hell do you want?"

"I was under the impression you were hunting for me," the tinny voice continued, and Roy bolted upright.

"I am hunting for some people right now. You never gave me your name."

"And I'm not going to, but I'll spend the next ten minutes answering your questions about the genetic alterations I worked on —the ones that ended abruptly seven years ago. The clock starts now, Agent. Pick wisely. Once I hang up, you'll never hear from me again."

Kincaid put the phone on speaker and hit the record function on his iPad. "Are any breeding farms left?"

"No."

"Are the products of your genetic manipulations a threat to humans?"

"Of course. You can do better than that, Agent."

Roy squeezed a pencil so hard it shattered in his hand. "Why are they a threat?"

"Because they have brains like high-powered computers, senses as sharp as any animal's, and physical prowess even the highest trained athlete can't come close to. If that's not enough, they can alter reality with their minds."

"You've told me what they can do, but why are they a threat?"

The scientist chortled. "Because they don't like humans at all. We created them to serve, and they decided they didn't want to anymore."

Roy glanced at the clock on his phone. Five minutes shot already. "Are they just in the U.S.?"

"Of course not."

"How many are there, roughly?"

"They could have bred more in the last seven years, but at the time of the rebellion, there were slightly over four thousand."

Roy whistled as shock pounded him. He'd been thinking a few hundred, perhaps a thousand at the most. Something else the scientist said registered. "You inferred that they're capable of reproduction."

"Of course. Their bodies are human, just augmented beyond your wildest imagination. One more minute, Agent. One more question."

"What do the females look like?"

"Why would you ask?"

Roy stared at the iPhone's display. Suddenly, he wondered if it was really a renegade scientist on the other end. He worded his answer carefully. "Because I've only killed the males."

"Yes, well, they guard their females carefully. All of them have black hair, but the females have green eyes. Time's up, Agent."

The connection went dead. Roy dropped the phone onto the bed and clicked off record on his iPad. He should send the transmission back to the mother ship, and he would, but not just yet.

Green eyes. Bile boiled into the back of his throat as the implication hit home.

Glory had green eyes. It might be coincidence. Or not. He'd never believed in coincidences. He bolted from the bed and paced from one side of the room to the other. What were the odds a scientist would track him down and answer even one question? Not very fucking good. All they wanted was to disappear. If the freaks found them, their number would be up.

That phone call had to come from freaks. It was the only explanation that made sense. They were tracking Glory, and had found him. He grabbed the phone and dialed the secure number to patch him through to HQ, telling the operator he needed a call traced from his cell. He wore a pattern in the carpet waiting until the technician came back online.

"No calls or texts have been registered either to or from your phone for the last hour, sir. There's been activity on your iPad, though."

"Thanks." Roy dropped the phone in his pocket and raked his hands through his hair. Freaks had called him, sounding him out. He shouldn't have asked about their females. He'd come up with a plausible explanation, but if they were as brilliant as they were supposed to be, whoever was on the other end would've seen right through him.

He drew the Sig, checked the clip, and shoved it back in its holster. Next he pulled the .32 snub nose from its ankle holster and did the same thing. Every single instinct at his disposal told him they needed to get moving. He pulled his side of the adjoining doors open and tapped gently on hers. When she didn't answer, he tapped louder.

Glory still didn't answer, so he pushed on the door, not surprised when the deadbolt's tongue defeated him. Cursing, he took a step back, aimed a kick, and the door splintered in its frame. He pushed his way through, expecting to hear an outraged yelp from her, but the room was empty.

Not quite believing what he saw, Roy checked both bathroom and closet before he raced back to his own room, stuffed his feet into his boots, and gathered his things. She didn't have that much of a head start. So long as a car didn't pick her up, he'd be able to find her.

He gritted his teeth together, vaulted from his room, and threw everything into the Toyota, hitting the clicker to lock it. What if something worse than a driver offering a ride got to her? Now that he knew what she was, he understood exactly who was chasing her.

Freaks. His nemesis.

He glanced at footsteps in the snow leading into a field. Thank Christ there was only a single set. Determination joined adrenaline as he pulled his Sig, undid the safety, and took off after her, running as fast as he could through knee deep drifts. His boots churned through the snow, and he focused his mind to melt the path in front of him so he could move faster.

CHAPTER 8

Glory crept through a snow-covered field dotted with trees and bushes. She'd left the motel half an hour before, as soon as she finished her hair and dried it with the blow dryer. She meant to wait until morning, but it was too risky. Roy might be an early riser. If he tapped on her door with a smile and coffee, she wouldn't have been able to resist. Plus, her finely-tuned brain told her Nameless Ones were close. They threw off an unmistakable oscillating frequency. She'd caught fragments of it when she emerged from the shower, and that had decided things.

Roy wouldn't figure out what she'd done until morning, which gave her a few hours' lead. Maybe by then, she'd have caught another ride and be miles away. She wanted to go back the way they'd come, but couldn't chance the roadblock again. She tapped into maps in her database brain, but couldn't come up with a viable southern route that didn't involve running the roadblock and going back through Hinckley. Once she made Duluth, she'd work on getting a ride east on Highway 2.

Glory stopped, scenting the air for clues. Did the Nameless Ones have a bead on her? Not yet, or they'd be closer. She chucked out more chaff to confuse them and eyed the highway. Was she far enough from the motel to risk exposing herself to thumb a ride? Maybe not quite yet. She remembered what Roy had said about tracking her footprints in the snow, but by the time he came after her, she'd be long gone.

She was grateful for the winter clothing. She still had Roy's parka. She'd been packed and ready to leave with his parka looped over a hook next to the door, but in the end she hadn't been able to abandon it. It smelled like him, and she craved the reminder of his kindness—and his hard-muscled body.

What would happen to her? She figured the Nameless Ones wouldn't give up, but she didn't expect them to up the ante, either. Would this be her life? Moving from one shadow to the next, always looking over her shoulder? She didn't like the answer, but didn't see how to change it, either. She could fake her death, but the Nameless Ones wouldn't be fooled for long.

As she trudged through snow as deep as her thighs in places, she puzzled over the locked gate in her mind, the one she couldn't defeat. She also thought about why the Nameless Ones kept such a tight rein on the women. She and her dorm mates kicked that can down the road many times. It was almost as if the Handlers were afraid if they didn't rule by fear, the women would escape their control.

Awesome if it's true, but what do we have that they don't?

She'd faced enough Nameless Ones in the arena to know she wasn't stronger than them. Maybe she was smarter, had a more nimble central processing unit. The thought made her smile. She didn't often let herself indulge in her hatred for the men who'd made her life hell for so long.

A shift in the air currents made her suddenly wary, and she faded into the shadows of a grove of leafless aspen trees. Glory had sworn not to use her power, but she needed it now. She sent her mind questing outward; subtle strands of consciousness sought the source of the anomaly.

Her heart stuttered in her chest as answers slammed into her.

Nameless Ones. At least half a dozen. They surrounded her and were closing fast. Obviously, they were onto her and had been chucking out chaff of their own to mask their presence. Her brain hit hyper drive as she ran every single possibility through to its conclusion.

All of them ended with her either dead or captured—unless she fought back hard, and even that was a crap shoot. Six or more to one were shit odds.

At least I have a choice—for once. I will never go back with them.

Courage blazed through her and she screamed. "Come and get me, you bastards."

She stripped off her thick gloves, and power crackled from her fingertips as she spun in a slow circle, scanning the darkness with her enhanced vision. The first man she saw would go up like a torch. And the second. She'd kill until they took her down, but first they had to get closer.

Much closer.

She tossed her shoulders back, fully expecting to be mowed down at any moment—if they'd brought guns. Without firepower, they killed the same way she did. Touch made it easier, but proximity would do. She threw everything wide open—every single enhanced sense quivered with anticipation as she pinpointed the Nameless Ones sent to bring her down. Light streamed from her like a beacon. It would make her easier to find, but who cared? She wanted them close enough to feel the bite of her vengeance.

Nameless Ones rushed her. She felt their distinctive energy signatures and stood her ground, shifting from foot to foot as she balanced power between her hands. She'd been right about there being six. A cold, detached calm descended and she sent killing blasts into three before they got close enough to damage her.

"You don't understand," blared in her mind. *"We don't want to kill you. We want to save you from the man. He's a danger to us all. That includes you. He captured you. We can't allow it."*

Running high on adrenaline, she didn't even blink. At least part of what the Nameless One said was true. Roy hated them as much as she did. She'd seen it in his mind. A saying she'd read lit up one of her neural circuits. Something about the enemy of her enemy being her friend.

Power rolled into her, singing her side, but not doing any real damage. She leaped backward and spun, ending up in a crouch she could defend. More white death flew from her hands. The fourth man sidestepped her first jolt of high-voltage rays, but she nailed him on her second try. Something different battered her enhanced senses from behind her. Before she could reposition herself to attack, Roy shouted, "Hit the ground, Glory. Now."

Trust came hard. She wouldn't have obeyed anyone else, but she dropped flat onto the snow. The detonation from his gun deafened her, and she shuttered her auditory function. Too late. Her ears resonated painfully.

Glory huddled in the snow. One more boom, and then nothing. Roy must have killed the last two. She waited, expecting him to shoot her next. He must have seen power arc from her hands. She'd had time to process what the Nameless One poured into her head. Roy was their enemy. Maybe he'd only been her friend because he didn't realize she was one of those he hunted.

Hands gripped her torso and hauled her upright. She sensed Roy's presence, felt heat pour off him, and cringed away. She couldn't look at him, see the disappointment—or worse revulsion—in his eyes. "Let me go. I was just leaving. They're dead—this bunch, anyway."

He folded her against him, and she smelled cordite and the masculine scent unique to him. Glory put up a token struggle, but finally gave in and let him hold her. He felt so good, he was impossible to walk away from.

"Come on," he said. "We need to put some distance between us and here."

"Why didn't you kill me too?"

He leaned back and looked at her. "Why would I want to do that?"

"Because you know what I am. You must have seen me kill the others."

He smoothed a gloved hand down her face. "I knew what you were when I came after you. Or I was pretty damned sure, anyway."

While Glory digested what that meant, she tugged her gloves out of a pocket and stuffed her fingers into them. "You know, and you don't mind?"

"It's deeper than that." He dropped a hand to her arm and linked it through. "Come on. At least you kill silently. Someone will have heard my gunshots, and I don't want to have to explain the bodies littering this field to anyone outside The Company. Got to call in so the closest cleanup crew can get here fast."

His words penetrated, and she loped back toward the motel and his car, listening to him give terse instructions over his cell. Nothing was left in her room, apparently not in his either, because he opened the Toyota's doors and gestured her inside. He gunned the engine, and they fishtailed out of the parking lot. "We'll need a different ride," he said, "but that can't happen before tomorrow. Tonight, best we can do is put as much distance as we can between us and here."

"You already said that."

"Bears repeating." He grinned at her. "Consider it your first lesson in fieldwork."

She settled into the passenger seat and took off her gloves and hat. It was scarcely her first lesson in fieldwork, but she kept her mouth shut. Her mind brimmed with questions, so she asked the logical one. "How'd you know I was gone?"

"I got a phone call…"

She listened while he relayed what had happened. He told the story as if it were a report, in logical order without any frills, much as she would've done. Once he finished talking, she said, "It was smart of you to deduce who called."

He pushed his jacket hood back and made a snorting noise. "What capped it was when I asked the mother ship to trace the call, and they came up dry. That was when I knew it couldn't be any of the renegade scientists. They're pretty much cut off from sophisticated technology at this point. Hell, none of them have so much as come up for air."

"A lot of them are dead. Maybe all."

He sat straighter. "Beyond the ones murdered during the rebellion?"

"Uh-huh. They were one of the first loose ends the Nameless Ones took care of."

"Why kill them? They created you."

Glory frowned. "You really don't know."

"I wouldn't have asked if I did." He adjusted the car's heater.

"Those like me are V3. Once the scientists didn't need V1 or 2 anymore, they killed them. That's what caused the rebellion seven years ago."

A sharp intake of breath told her Roy had no idea how cruel and uncaring her creators had been. "Why not make use of them?" he asked. "Surely they weren't that different from you?"

She pressed her tongue against her teeth, thinking, sorting what to tell him. "They didn't teach us much about our origins, but enough so we'd hate humans and work hard to subvert them. Some of the older Nameless Ones had friends in the V1 and 2 batches. Losing them scarred them."

"What about the women?"

"If there were women much older than me, I never met them, but the compound where I lived was huge, and there were parts I never saw. Plus, it wasn't the only one. Groups of us are scattered all over."

"Do you know where?"

"No. The Handlers used us for missions, but didn't ever tell us much." She smirked remembering *need to know basis* lectures.

"How come you have a name, and the men don't?" Roy drummed

his fingers on the steering wheel. "There's so much I want to know, I'm not certain where to start asking questions."

"You've asked a pile so far. What makes you so sure I'll answer any more of them?" Glory narrowed her eyes and looked at his profile illuminated by the lighted dashboard. She'd be wise to titrate what information she shared until she determined if he'd be willing to spare the women, at least the ones she knew. Maybe the rest of them too.

"Because you hate those fuckers as much as I do. By my count, you've killed five now." He shot an appraising glance her way.

"I still think your best bet is to let me out of the car in the middle of Duluth and go on with whatever you were doing when you met me." The words cost her, and her gut clenched in protest. If he had her enhanced senses, he'd sense the pain behind those words. Understand that leaving him was the last thing she wanted.

"You're just being noble. Cut it out." His deep, rumbly voice soothed her like a balm.

"How would you know?"

"Because I'm more like you than you realize. When it was obvious we were losing, I had the CDC lab cook up an infusion that makes humans more like you. I was the guinea pig, but when the concoction didn't kill me, I advised my team to take it too."

"Isn't that like some sort of civil rights violation?"

"Smart cookie. Yeah, I couldn't force them, so I found replacements for the men who balked."

Glory cleared her throat. "Even if you've bewitched me, I still know it'd be safer for you if I weren't here."

"I already told you I don't care about that." His voice roughened. "I care about you, and I know you feel the same. You can't fake what I sensed when you were in my arms."

"Sometimes people walk away from those they care for to keep them safe. I've seen it in movies," she insisted. "And I've read up on human nature. The Handlers insisted we learn everything we could about humans, so we'd have a psychological edge understanding them."

"I'm not leaving until you tell me you're sick of my sorry ass. Got it?"

A laugh burbled past her lips. It surprised her almost as much as the tears had. "Got it."

"You never answered me about names."

"The girls and I named ourselves. We got tired of numbers. The men probably have names, but they never told us what they were, so we called them Nameless Ones. Pretty soon, it's what they called themselves."

"Why'd you pick Glory?" Curiosity sharpened his words.

"Because it gave me hope. It means great admiration, honor, or praise I can earn by brave deeds."

He reached across the center divider and grasped her hand. "It also means great beauty."

Warmth began in her belly and radiated outward, and she squeezed his hand, wanting to tell him that he was the glorious one, but she was too uncertain of how he'd take it to get the words out.

To cover her confusion, she asked. "What did you mean by mother ship? Does the CIA operate a space station?"

Roy laughed; the sound warmed her. "Nah, it's just my special name for headquarters. I stuck with using it because it pisses off the man I work for."

Glory digested the information. Apparently in Roy's world, people weren't punished for insubordination. At least not small infractions.

A COLORLESS DAWN lightened the sky as they passed through Duluth. He'd stopped for coffee and breakfast sandwiches at a convenient Starbucks and for fuel. He'd also called HQ, filled them in further on last night's problems, and arranged for someone to meet them with a different car about twenty miles outside the city limits, along Lake Superior's southern shore.

Glory dozed off and on. She was asleep again now, which was good. She looked trashed with black smudges beneath her eyes. The lighter hair suited her, made her more gamine than waif. He'd tried to draw her out about any residual guilt around killing the freaks, but she'd remained silent.

He'd gathered more intel on his pet project in the few hours they'd been in the car than he'd picked up from years in the field. As they'd talked, he hatched a plan. The best and safest place for Glory was in Langley, Virginia in a safe house where agents could rotate guard duty 24/7. He hadn't floated that idea. Not yet, anyway. She was still harping on her crackpot scheme about leaving to keep him safe, but at least she hadn't said brought it up in the last half hour before she fell asleep.

Roy tamped down rising excitement. He finally had what he needed to win, to push the freaks off the fucking map—forever. He closed his teeth over his lower lip. How much help Glory gave him from here on had to be her choice. Much as he wanted to, he refused to push her. She might hate her Handlers, but they were still her people, and she was savvy enough to realize every piece of intel she shared was a nail in the freaks' coffins. She seemed genuinely fond of the women she'd shared housing with. Maybe there might be a way to salvage them, and the other females as well. They'd make a hell of a commando unit—fighting for the right side.

He chuckled softly.

"What?" she asked, her voice saturated with sleep.

"You looked like a damned Valkyrie out there in the snowy field. I've never seen such precision killing. Light streamed from you, like you were some magical creature out of a legend."

Her eyes snapped open, and she plucked her cup of coffee from its holder and swallowed. "The light's a corollary of when I throw everything wide open, an electrical field. The men don't glow like that, and I never understood why."

"Maybe we can figure it out together. Off the cuff, it could mean you're stronger than them. Regardless, you still looked like a goddess. It was all I could do not to drop to my knees and worship you."

Glory rolled her eyes. "I'm guessing that's a compliment. Even though they trained me to kill, it still feels wrong." She sipped more coffee, and her forehead crinkled in confusion.

He understood, better than she could imagine, and he weighed his next words carefully. "It's the hardest part of the work I do. You don't ever want to get used to it. Once you do, you cross a line and become something less than human."

She put her coffee down and wrapped her arms around herself. "Do you think about who you've killed?"

Roy nodded. "Every single person. They never go away." He swallowed and forced himself to keep talking because she needed to hear it. "It's why I never signed up for missions where we'd drop munitions from an airplane, or set bombs to detonate. I didn't want to be in a position of killing where I couldn't control who or when."

"You've worked with men who've done those kinds of things."

It wasn't a question. He glanced at her. "You can read my mind, can't you?"

"Yes." An uncomfortable look screwed her features into a sheepish expression. "Not that I'd snoop now, but before I knew if I could trust you, I looked around, but only a little."

"It's okay. I have nothing to hide, at least not from you. Why'd you ask about men with a taste for blood?"

"I want to understand them better." She thinned her lips into a line. "Everything I know about humans comes from the Internet, television, and movies."

"Your genetic basis is human," he pointed out gently.

Glory nodded. "Even more reason I should know more than I do."

"Espionage is a weird business. Very few agents lead normal lives. Most leave a trail of broken marriages. Some drink too much.

Killing eats away at a piece of your humanity." He blew out a breath. "We tell ourselves we're the hedge keeping the free world free, but the bottom line is we're a bunch of adrenaline junkies who enjoy living on the ragged edge. Some of us really get off on killing, but most of us don't. I've weeded out the trigger happy ones so they're not part of my cohorts."

"This is one of the first conversations I've ever had where I haven't felt information was being titrated." She reached across the divider, and he gripped her hand.

"You're welcome. I'm going to stop at that gas station just ahead."

"But we already got fuel."

"You're going to rustle up those contact lenses of yours and put them in. I don't want the field agent who meets us with the car asking questions."

"You're not going to blow my cover?" Incredulity underscored her words.

Roy pulled into the service station, brought the car to a halt, and smiled at her. "No, Glory. If and when that happens, it will be your choice."

"What happens after we swap cars?"

"We find a deserted country road. I'm going to teach you to drive. And we're going to find out if I can manage that neat trick where you kill someone by shooting lightning at them."

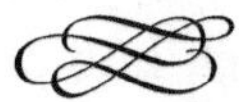

CHAPTER 9

To her unpracticed eye, the new car didn't look much different from the last one. It was another dark-colored SUV, but this one had a GMC logo. The storm, which had abated slightly, returned in force, and Roy made a couple quick recoveries once they began to skid. She watched what he did as he drove, filing the various parts away and interpreting the interplay between the transmission selection and his foot moving between accelerator and brake pedals.

"Think you can do this?" His voice broke into her concentration.

"Yes. All I needed was a pattern to observe. I would have taken a car from the compound if I'd known more."

"Wouldn't have helped you."

"Why not?"

"I'll bet they have GPS tracker units in their cars. We do."

"Oh." She chewed on her lower lip. "Should've thought about that. I watched enough spy stories on the Internet." Glory hesitated a beat. "What happens next?"

"That depends entirely on you." He swerved the big car to the right and they bumped down a side road with deep drifts. He stopped and jockeyed the four wheel drive lever until a light reading *Four Low* flashed into being on the dashboard.

Because it was easier than thinking about the future, she said, "I'm ready to try."

He got out and walked around the car. She scrambled over the divider and adjusted the seat like she'd seen him do when they first got into the car. Glory glanced at the dashboard, saw a flashing red light, and snapped her seatbelt into place, gratified when the light went out.

Roy got inside, closed his door, and buckled in, chucking softly. "What's so funny?"

"One of the big plusses of me never having kids was I thought I'd get out of having to teach them to drive."

"Is it that hard? Doesn't seem like it."

"Depends on the kid. I've heard horror stories from buddies. Hang onto the wheel just tight enough to feel the road beneath the tires, and feed it a little gas after you've looked around to make certain no other cars are close."

She curled her fingers around the wheel; it was still warm from his hands. "I haven't seen another car since we turned down this side road."

"True, but if you develop good habits now—"

"Save the lecture for after I fuck up."

He snorted laughter. "Fair enough."

Glory sent her senses through her fingertips. Breath whistled against her teeth once she realized she had a huge and unexpected edge in this driving game.

"What is it?" Roy peered through the blowing storm. "Did you see something? Are more of those bastards close by?"

"Nothing like that. The car. It has a computer."

He leaned back against his seat. "All the new cars have them." He snapped his fingers. "You can communicate with it."

"Uh-huh. Let's see if it helps. Maybe it can tell me things like which gear I need or if the wheels are getting close to skidding."

The next half hour sped past. By the time it was over, she was confident she could drive any car with a computer under damn near any conditions. The car became an extension of her enhanced senses, and she almost didn't need to see to guide it down the road.

"I'm impressed," Roy said, "but you need to get back in the passenger seat."

"Why? I'm doing great." She pulled the car to a halt as close to the deep drifts next to the side of the road as she dared.

"Yes, you are, but we'll be getting back on a main road, and you don't have a driver's license."

Circuitry clicked in her mind. "I can't get one without identification, huh?" Her earlier feelings of hopelessness threatened to break through. She pushed her door open, and walked around to the passenger side. This time, it was Roy who climbed over the divider and settled into the driver's seat.

"Why bother to teach me to drive," she demanded once she was back inside, "if I can't ever use the skill?"

He turned to face her, and cupped the side of her head with a hand. "No skills are ever wasted, but what makes you think you can't get a license?"

"No ID."

He patted her face. "I work for the CIA. Remember? We're experts at things like that. I have several sets of identification, in case one of my identities gets blown."

"Is Roy Kincaid your real name?"

"One of them."

She waited until he slipped the car into gear and turned them back toward the highway. It was clear he wasn't going to say more. "Trust happens in layers, doesn't it?"

"I've never heard it put quite that way, but yes."

She shut her eyes for a moment. When she opened them, she retreated to her earlier question. "What happens next?"

He glanced at the dashboard clock. "It's midafternoon. We drive until dinnertime, and then we'll find a place to eat and stop for the night."

"Yes, but where are we going?"

"Where do you want to go, Glory? Where were you heading when I found you?"

It was a big question, and she had an equally complex answer. "I didn't mean to leave the compound quite so soon. I was waiting, biding my time—"

"So you meant to try to escape sometime?" he cut in.

"Yes. Me and the girls, we were going to figure out something together."

"The man who tried to hurt you forced your hand."

She nodded. "I'd never used my ability to kill before. If I had, I might have trusted modulating it, so I only knocked him unconscious. He'd have gotten in trouble for dragging me to his room, and the others might not have punished me." She drew in a ragged breath. "Once he was dead though, I knew I had to leave."

"Maybe your subconscious was driving things."

"What do you mean?" She glanced at him to read his expression, which was stone-cold serious.

"You wanted to leave, but were afraid, so you inadvertently set things up to narrow your choices. I've done the same thing more than once."

She considered his words. "You might be onto something. Anyway, there were lots of things I needed to get squared away before I left, and none of them happened."

"You haven't told me why you wanted out of there."

"No, guess I haven't." She shrugged self-consciously, not sure what she wanted to reveal. "Aside from the obvious where the Nameless Ones used us for their purposes—"

"What purposes?" he broke in again as he swung the car back onto Highway 2.

"Stop interrupting me." Irritation burned a path through her, but she batted it aside. "Let me tell you the parts I want to. Once I'm done, you can ask questions, but I may not answer them."

"Touché. Sorry. Buy hey, we're in this together. You've got to trust me if this is going to work."

Rather than defending her skittishness, she launched into what seemed safe to tell him. "I don't have any memories from before the rebellion. None of the women did. The main reason I wanted out of there was to see if I could discover a way to unlock my mind. It's like there's a gate mechanism, but I don't have the key." She realized she'd laced her fingers together in her lap so hard they hurt, and she relaxed the pressure.

"What'd you hope remembering would buy you?" Roy's voice was gentle.

"I thought if I could remember, then I'd understand—everything. Like what happened to those like me. Something beyond the canned explanation of us being V3 and hating the humans who killed off the versions before."

He didn't say anything, so she hurried on. "I wasn't even totally clear until right before I escaped that I came from a lab and not someone's home. I wanted to find out where that lab was. Who'd engineered me. Hell," she bit her lip so hard she tasted blood, "I'm not even sure about what I can do. The Handlers kept designing new tasks for us."

He drew his brows together. "Maybe they didn't know, either."

Shock roiled through her and puzzle pieces clicked into place. That might explain why they kept the women under such ironclad control.

"You just figured something out," Roy said. "Care to tell me what?"

"The men were afraid of us. Not that they'd ever admit it, but it's the only explanation for why they kept us corralled. What you said about them not knowing the full extent of our abilities resonated. Felt like truth."

"It's not snowing quite so heavily. Want to test your theory?" He glanced her way and quirked a brow.

"How?"

"Let's see if you can teach me about that lightning trick. I'm enough like the freaks, I should be able to master it."

She grimaced. "I hate the Nameless Ones too, but I wish you wouldn't call them that. It makes me feel dirty."

Contrition pinched the skin around his eyes into a series of fine lines. "I'm sorry. Long habit, but of course you're right. You're part of them, and when I use a derogatory name it drags you down too."

"Thanks for understanding. Let me talk you through how I access the part of me that I used to kill those men."

ROY FLEXED his fingers one more time. They were in a deserted, snow-covered field somewhere past the Minnesota-Wisconsin line, shielded by a thick grove of evergreen trees. Despite the chill of the fading day, sweat ran down his body. He clamped his jaws together. "I'm going to try this one more time."

Glory cocked her head to one side. "You're doing everything I said? Not skipping steps?"

"No, I didn't *skip any steps.*" He heard annoyance in his voice and was quick to add, "That was snarky. I'm just frustrated."

"I would be too. Once I tap into the motor center in my cerebral cortex, everything else just follows."

He stared at his bare fingers, white from cold, and then at hers, which were still rosy from power funneling through them. "You may be onto something about males reacting differently to the gene splicing that created you."

Her face kindled with curiosity. "Do you know what they did? How they made us?"

He shook his head, and guilt smote him when her excited expression evaporated. "No. When I met you, I was hunting for the scientists because we need answers. From what you said, I was on the biggest wild goose chase of them all."

"I really don't believe any of them are left, but I'm not a hundred percent positive." She gestured for him to get on with things.

Roy agreed since his hands were numb. He shut his eyes, threw the augmented center in his brain wide open and funneled electrical impulses through his hands. Muted crackling teased his ears, and an anemic flash illuminated his right hand.

"Yes." She was by his side in an instant. "Do it again, but give it more juice and use the other side of your brain too. Remember, right side controls left body."

He shot her a crooked smile. "What if there isn't any more *juice?*"

"There has to be," she insisted and her eyes widened. "I have an idea. Let me link with you. Maybe I can kick those pathways into action."

He hesitated, but not for long. "Go for it." He met her gaze and left himself open. Once she was fully inside his mind, she could kill him, but he didn't think she would.

If she wanted me dead, she could have taken me out any time.

"Let me know if it's too much." Something warm and vibrant settled behind his forehead.

"How will I do that?"

She grinned. "You won't have to do a thing because I'll know every single one of your thoughts, probably before you do."

He drew back, thinking of secrets he'd buried deep and held for years. "Maybe this isn't such a good idea."

She looked at him askance. "I won't tap your memory, only what's happening now."

He raked a hand through his hair. She was already inside his head. If she stumbled over the massacre he'd masterminded in the Middle East, so be it. Years had passed, and he'd come to terms with it—almost.

"I'm game. Let's get this show rolling. It'll be dark soon."

She didn't answer, but he felt a jolt as she pressed deeper into his mind, joining with him. *"Try it now."* Her voice prodded from within. *"Pay attention to what's different."*

He felt doors in his mind being prodded open, one after the other. He'd only tapped two; she blew triple that number down. When he looked at his body, it glowed with the same soft light pouring off her, and understanding brought a fierce smile to his face.

Roy imagined electricity streaming through him, firing from his hands, and saw light arc twenty feet. Snow melted from nearby bushes, and they began to smolder. Excitement beat a path from his brain to his boots, and the arc widened to forty feet. When he raised his gaze to Glory's face, her smile matched his own.

"Yes!" She fist pumped the air and extricated her energy from his mind. "Try it without me."

All the circuitry was still engaged. He couldn't manage more than twenty feet on his own, but it was good enough. Something to build on. Roy felt like whooping wildly, but he restrained himself, shut down the neural pathways, remembering where each one was, and scooped Glory into his arms. "Thank you."

"Thank you for taking a chance." She burrowed against him. "It will get easier, but you need practice."

"No kidding. Not quite ready to give up my Sig yet." He would have patted it where it hung in its shoulder holster, but he didn't want to let go of Glory.

"This is another benefit." Her voice brushed across his mind.

Wonder filled him. He'd tried telepathic communication with his men once they'd had the injections, but either no one heard him, or it scared the living shit out of them, and they hadn't answered. He tightened his hold on her and pushed with his mind. *"Can you hear me?"*

"Of course, silly."

He nuzzled her neck, kissing warm flesh, and she turned her mouth to meet his. Unlike their first kiss, which had begun tentatively, this one started at Mach speed and took off from there.

She threaded her fingers beneath his hair and clung to his scalp. He pushed his tongue against her teeth, and she opened her mouth to his kiss, sucking hungrily on his tongue.

Roy cupped the curves of her ass and snugged her against his growing erection. It'd been months since he'd been with a woman, and lust clawed him like a live thing. It was tempting to push her into the snow, rip her pants out of the way, and shove into her. She ground her hips against him and made a sensual, moaning noise deep in her throat.

He broke away from their kiss, his breath coming fast, and his cock on the verge of coming. "Not here," he managed.

She moved a hand between them and curved it around his cock. "I want to see what you look like. I've never…" She faltered, "Outside of pictures, that is." Color splotched across her face, and her nipples were hard points against his chest even through their layers of clothing.

"I want to see you naked too, sweetheart. For that we need a motel."

"We have the car." She glanced at the SUV.

He'd thought of it too and discarded it. "Not for your first time. I want a bed. I want to pleasure you, not fumble beneath your clothes in the backseat."

"Okay." Her flush deepened, and he wondered if she was embarrassed about being so forward, but then she shot a coquettish look his way, and he chalked her color up to arousal, pure and simple. "Don't say I didn't offer."

He let go of her reluctantly and rearranged his straining cock so it wasn't bent double. She patted the front of his pants. "Looks uncomfortable. I could—"

He grabbed her hand and held it tight in his. "We do this together or not at all."

CHAPTER 10

Roy watched the gentle swing of Glory's hips as they returned to the SUV. Maybe because they'd shared something even more intimate than sex, he felt they were already lovers. Once they settled in the car, the muted beep of his phone told him he needed to check messages. He scrolled through, listening and reading texts. By the time he was done, battle mode had displaced lust.

"What is it?" she asked.

"Freaks, er Nameless Ones launched attacks. The CDC in Atlanta is a smoking ruin. So's Johns Hopkins Research Center."

"Why target them?"

"Because that's where we resurrected the research projects that spawned those like you. It's one of the reasons I was hunting for any remaining scientists. So they could help."

She gazed at her hands, looking guilty.

"I'm not going to push, but if you know something, anything at all, I could use it."

Glory met his gaze. She still wore her contact lenses and her hazel eyes looked troubled. "I don't know anything, not for sure, but the only assignment I ever did for the Nameless Ones happened the same night I left."

Questions thundered through Roy, but he forced them back, waiting for what she'd tell him. His long career pushing, prodding, and dragging information out of the unwilling wasn't useful right now.

After a pause so long he nearly chewed a hole in his cheek, she said, "I stole data from a company. I didn't look at what I downloaded, but it might have included those sites. They're the kind of thing the Nameless Ones would want to know." Glory swallowed hard. "Did they take anything from those labs, or just blow them to hell?"

"We don't know." He pinched the bridge of his nose between his thumb and forefinger. "I have to go back to Langley. They need me to activate my team."

"I understand." She nodded solemnly. "You can leave me off somewhere between here and there."

"The fuck I will." He reached across the car and grabbed her shoulders. "Don't you get it? I'm never leaving you anywhere. Not if I can help it."

A soft smile curved her lips. "That's the nicest thing anyone's ever said to me, but you're not being practical. You have to work. What would I do?"

Reality crashed hard, and Roy shook himself. "Let me think about it. I'll come up with something. In the meantime, how far away does telepathic speech work?"

She drew her brows together, thinking. "I'm not sure. At least over a quarter mile. It might be more robust, but no one told me, and I never tested it."

Ideas rattled through his head as he drove south on Highway 51, heading for Dane County Regional Airport where a chopper would pick him up. If he called HQ and told them about Glory, he had no doubt they'd approve transporting her too, but he'd promised her he wouldn't blow her cover. If they could communicate telepathically over distance, it might make leaving her a little more palatable—but not much.

"Talk to me," she said after he'd been silent for the better part of half an hour. "I'm starting to feel lonely over here."

"Not sure what to say." Roy scrunched his forehead until it hurt. No matter what, he wouldn't put any pressure on her. Christ! She'd spent her entire life at someone else's beck and call. How could he do the same thing to her?

"You're running scenarios in your head. Talk them through with me."

When he glanced sidelong at her, she was looking right at him, her heart in her eyes. He rotated his shoulder blades to relieve the steel bar of tension sitting between them, and she snaked a hand behind his neck and rubbed his stiff muscles.

"God, but that feels good." He leaned into her touch.

"Talk to me, Roy. Let me help. I have a very good mind."

The corners of his mouth twitched. "I know you do." Half a snort escaped. "If the Nameless Ones hadn't been so gun shy of you and the other women, they could have made more use of you."

Her eyes twinkled. "I'll bet you could do a much better job."

"Yes. No. Aw, shit. That didn't come out right." Roy took the next exit. It would make him late to the rendezvous, but the bird wouldn't leave without him. When he saw a deserted building with a plowed parking lot, he pulled into it and shut off the ignition.

"Did you change your mind about the backseat?" She furled her brows and jerked a hand behind them.

"Be serious. We have to talk, and there's not much time. Do you want to come with me?"

She threaded her fingers together and rested her chin on her hands, twisting so she could look at him. "I'm of two minds. Part of me still thinks you'd be better off without me, but after what you said about the strikes on those research centers, I started thinking I might do more good if you let me be a part of your response to the attacks."

"Keep talking." He thought he knew where she was going, but she needed to say it, not him.

"I understand the Nameless Ones better than any of you." She stopped looking at him and examined something on the floor. "Maybe if I help you, someone you work with could figure out how to unlock that place in my head."

Understanding washed through him. That's why she looked so uncomfortable. She wasn't used to asking for anything, let alone bargaining.

"I was going to offer that anyway," he said. "Does that mean you want to come with me?" At her nod, he went on. "I'd draft you as a civilian special agent, which means you'd be with me, working on my team, but you'd still be in danger. I'll lay down my life to keep you safe, but there aren't any guarantees in this work."

"I'm in danger now," she said, and managed to meet his gaze again. "I ran our coordinates through the map program in my head, and I assume we're headed for Madison. If I don't go with you, there's a big university there where I could probably blend in, at least for a while."

The thought of being separated from her was painful, and Roy didn't understand it. Day before yesterday, she hadn't been so much as a blip on his radar screen. Was he so isolated from the female half of the species that the first proximity in ages turned him into a lapdog?

It doesn't matter. If I don't speak up and something happens to her, I'll never forgive myself.

"I don't want you to do that," he said. "You still don't have any ID. No cell phone, although that's easy enough if I gave you money." He quieted, organizing his thoughts, figuring out where exactly to pigeonhole her if he moved his emotions off the scoreboard. She gave him space, waiting with an expectant look while she rubbed his neck and shoulders again.

He leveled his gaze at her. "The way I see this, you're kind of like a specialized life form, one we want to protect, and one who has special skills that could help us. Protocol in that instance is moving you close to the mother ship and putting you up in a special company apartment with 24/7 guards watching over you."

She knit her brows together. "It sounds like I'd be just as much a prisoner as I was back in Washington State."

He'd wondered where she came from. Now he knew. "It's a bit off topic, but you'll have to show us where in Washington, so we can activate a team to help your friends who are still there."

Her eyes sheened with sudden tears. "You'd do that for me?"

"Of course."

"Hope, Charity, Faith…Hell, all of them. They'd be so grateful."

The names smote Roy's heart. Deprived of basic human rights, the women had chosen to call themselves something inspirational. "As soon as HQ clears up the mess from the CDC and Johns Hopkins, I'll do my damnedest to authorize things to get a team headed their way."

"I have to go with them."

He started to say no. Instead, he asked, "Why?"

"Because the women trust me. Otherwise, they might hurt your men. They can all do exactly what I can—kill with their thoughts."

"Good point." He blew out a breath. "We have a lot to do in a relatively short time. If you're certain about coming with me, I'll put in a call to let them know, and so they can get some ID cooking for you. Mind if I take a picture?"

Glory straightened and faced him while he snapped two headshots with his phone and forwarded them to the CIA's documents unit.

"What will my last name be?" she asked.

"They'll surprise you. Your first name will be different too."

"No. I want to keep my name. I didn't have one for too long."

Roy grinned. "Okay. We'll make you two sets of ID. You'll probably need that, anyway."

He keyed in Langley's number and asked for his boss. For once in his long and distinguished career, Milton Edward Reins III was at a loss for words, but the lapse didn't last long. When he began rattling off plans for Glory, Roy cut him off. "We'll talk once we get there."

Satisfied he'd done all he could, he headed the car back toward the highway. "How are you feeling?" he asked.

"Not sure. Lots of conflicting things," she replied. "Excited. Scared. Wondering if I'm doing the right thing."

Roy smiled. "You wouldn't be human if you didn't feel all those things."

"But I'm not—not exactly, anyway."

"Maybe you're more human than you know." He blew out a breath and reached across to grip her hand. "When I was a boy, I inhaled science fiction and fantasy books. Still enjoy them when I get time to read, which isn't often. I always believed we'd come up with a race of super humans. It was one of the reasons I volunteered for the injections to make me more like the freaks."

He grimaced. "Damn it! Sorry. It will take me a while to retrain my vocabulary."

She stroked the back of his hand. "It's okay. I shouldn't be so sensitive. These injections. Are they permanent?"

He nodded. "There were a series. Six of them, but afterward the effects weren't reversible. Obviously, they didn't confer all the advantages you have, but they did sharpen my senses." He furrowed his brow, thinking. "Given what happened just a little bit ago, I'm guessing I've barely scratched the surface of what changed in me."

She gazed out the windshield. "Good. I want you to be like me."

Something warm and unfamiliar fluttered in Roy's belly. Feelings waking up after being suffocated, bundled, and tossed on the slagheap for years. It felt scary, but he welcomed them anyway. Caring for Glory would make him vulnerable, but he yearned for her touch, her voice, the feel of her in his arms.

No going back. Got to play this through to the endgame.

~

THEY REACHED the airport an hour later, and headed for the heliport tucked off to one side of the main passenger terminal. Glory got out and opened the backdoor to retrieve the backpack Roy had bought her. He plucked his things from the space behind the backseat.

"Do we need to do something with the car?" she asked.

"I'll slide the keys under the floor mats. An agent will be by soon to pick it up."

"There must be a lot of you."

"Not so many, but we're well organized. Come on. You're about to meet Charlie, one of my team."

She trotted next to Roy, matching his long-legged stride as they headed for a sleek, black helicopter with double rotors that spun slowly. A man detached himself from the craft, bent to avoid the prop wash, and vaulted toward them. He looked a lot like Roy. Tall, thickly muscled with dark hair, and dressed in a black jacket and black pants. His nose was uneven, probably from being broken, and a scar ran from his left cheekbone down to his chin. Once he got close enough, she saw a pair of mischievous, brown eyes.

"Son of a bitch," he said. "Never thought that hunting expedition of yours would yield shit." He ground to a halt in front of them, forcing them to stop too.

Glory felt Charlie's scrutiny and held herself a little straighter. She was starting a new life with a clean slate, and it felt important she not be found wanting—on any front. She wriggled her glove off and extended a hand. "Hello. I'm Glory."

He grasped her hand, continuing his frank appraisal. "Charlie McClaren."

"You're staring," Roy observed.

"Yeah, well." Charlie shrugged. "It's the first time I've seen a female freak."

Her stomach tightened. She wanted to slug him, but clamped her jaws together instead and jerked her hand from his grasp.

The corners of Charlie's generous mouth curved into a broad grin. "Temperamental little vixen, isn't she?"

Roy opened his mouth, probably to defend her, but Glory jumped in before he had a chance. She crossed her arms under her breasts and said, "Now look here. I don't want to get off on the wrong foot, but I'd take it as a kindness if you wouldn't refer to me as a freak. And if you're going to talk about me as if I'm not here, I'll call you on that too."

Charlie jabbed Roy in the side. "See. She is temperamental."

Glory grabbed his arm and forced him to look at her. "I'm right here. Don't talk about me as if I'm miles away. You'd be *temperamental* too if someone did that to you."

Charlie looked as if he'd bitten into a rotten peach just before he burst out laughing. "You got me good, sister." He stepped aside and made a sweeping bow in the direction of the helicopter. "Welcome to my chariot. Care for a ride?"

Her annoyance evaporated, and she quirked a brow. "Are you always like this?"

"Usually, he's worse," Roy said. "Let's roll. We're late as it is."

"No shit." Charlie loped toward the chopper. "Watch your head," he called over one shoulder.

She crawled up the steps into the helicopter and sat where Roy indicated in the second row of seats. Unlike the pilot and copilot seats, hers faced the center of the craft. Roy took the right front seat, Charlie the left.

"If you want to talk with us, you'll have to put on a headset," Roy said and handed her a moss green pair. "Push this button when you have something you want to say." He pointed to the microphone stem jutting from the headset.

"Got it." She settled the contraption over her head and heard a muted hum. Glory took in her surroundings. She'd never flown before, and her stomach wasn't certain she'd like it. The helicopter had sixteen seats. Floor bolts suggested they could be easily removed, which would free the craft to carry cargo. Charlie pulled the door shut, and her tummy did a little flip-flop.

Don't be ridiculous. This will be easy. Just like driving in a car, except we're in the air.

The rotor noise intensified, even through her headset, and she dialed her auditory function back a few notches. The craft bolted skyward and headed southeast. Conversation was sparse, and she watched the men trade off piloting the craft. "Can all of you fly?"

"Most of us," Roy answered.

"I could do it too," she said. "I've been watching. There are a few more buttons and knobs than in the car, but the principles are similar, and I believe I understand each of them. Is there a manual handy that I could read?"

The line of Charlie's jaw tightened, and he gripped the yoke hard enough to make his knuckles turn white.

"What'd I say?" Glory asked. "I didn't mean to give offense."

Roy turned to face her, his expression serious. "We've been fighting your kind for seven years. One of our fears was because you're smarter and stronger, we'd lose and—"

"I get that," she broke in. "What does that have to do with flying this thing?" She slapped the aluminum skin next to her.

"Flying is harder than driving. A lot harder. And flying helicopters is tougher than flying airplanes because there aren't wings to provide stability. When you said it wouldn't be a problem for you, Charlie probably—"

"I can talk for myself," Charlie said gruffly. "Sorry, Glory. You'll take some getting used to. It will take time before the men trust you."

Her mind shuffled through possibilities. "Would any of them try to hurt me because they were scared?"

"Maybe—" Charlie began.

"Not on my watch." Roy spoke over him.

Charlie shot an odd glance sidelong at his team leader, but kept his mouth shut.

Glory slumped against her seat. Suddenly, the road ahead didn't feel as predictable as it had talking with Roy in the car. She hadn't counted on humans distrusting her.

I'm different. What did I expect? That they'd welcome me with open arms? Even I'm not quite that naïve.

CHAPTER 11

The next week passed in a blur of clothes, ID tags, weaponry practice, and a slew of new faces and names. Doctors prodded her, examined her, and took MRI imagery of every part of her body. She hardly saw Roy at all, but they talked several times a day on her brand new cell phone. Her apartment was lovely. At first she couldn't believe the three rooms plus bath were all for her.

Her quarters had a living room with a plush, tan faux-leather sofa and two matching chairs arranged around an oak coffee table and flat screen television. The kitchen had a chiller, microwave, and a real stove with an oven. Her bedroom held a double bed piled with pillows and blankets. She still couldn't wrap her mind around having more than one of each. She'd often slept with all her clothes on, huddled beneath her single blanket at the compound, and still felt cold.

But the bathroom was the best. It had a bathtub deep enough to truly soak in and inexhaustible hot water. She'd been limited to three minute showers before, and even then the water had edged toward cold halfway into her allotted time. Fluffy towels, scented soap, and a full length mirror on the back of the door made her feel like she'd died and awakened a princess.

Clothes had materialized. So many the bedroom closet and dresser were mostly full. She had field clothes, dress clothes, and four more pair of shoes in addition to the boots Roy bought her.

Roy.

Glory walked to the barred window and stared out at the bustle of the CIA compound. The sky was just lightening with the first rays of dawn. The helicopter had touched down on the roof of one of the buildings, and she hadn't left The Company's protective fold since. A soft tap sounded on her door, startling her. Granted the CIA never slept, but who could possibly need her at this hour? Usually, no one came for her much before nine. She glanced at her schedule laying on the coffee table. Today she was slated for a ten-mile run, more weapons practice, and yet one more doctor appointment. She rolled her eyes. So far, the medical staff hadn't told her a damned thing. She was getting close to just peeking into their heads and calling it even.

The tap sounded again. She dragged her robe tighter around her body and walked to the door, tugging it open. Roy stood there in full battle regalia, with ammo belts crisscrossed over his chest. Rather than black, his pants and jacket were camouflage. He cocked his head to one side. "Are you going to invite me in?"

Glory shook herself. It was so good to see him in the flesh, she'd been standing there like a dolt just drinking him in. She stepped aside, feeling her face heat. "Of course." She motioned to him, and he pushed the door shut with a booted foot. Why didn't he open his arms to invite her into a hug?

She licked suddenly dry lips. Her body, naked beneath her robe, came alive, sensitized to his presence. "It's good to see you," she ventured. "I've missed you."

"We've talked every day."

She narrowed her eyes. Why'd he sound defensive? "Sure, but it's not the same as having you here. Every night, I've hoped..."

Something in his eyes stopped her, and her words trailed to nothingness.

"We have to talk." He moved to the sofa and sat, lacing his fingers together in his lap.

"Sure." She sat next to him. "It looks like you're on your way to maneuvers."

"The team's been deployed. We'll be gone for a few days. Maybe as much as a week."

Truth slammed into her. "You can't go without me. You said you'd make me a civilian agent. You promised—" She heard the whining tone in her voice and stopped talking.

He shut his eyes for a moment. "I tried. Uncle Miltie refused. After the third time, he told me not to bring it up again."

"Who's Uncle Miltie?"

"Milton Reins III. The man who runs the CIA."

Roy tugged his hands apart and reached for hers. "Even though I never said a word about being so taken with you that you're all I can think about, I'm sure Miltie figured it out. He's the one who recruited me thirteen years ago, and he knows me really well. He lectured me about treating all my team members equally, not putting anyone at risk because I was trying to protect someone special." Roy exhaled sharply. "Even though he talked in generalities, his message came through loud and clear."

Glory yanked her hands out of Roy's. She didn't want to let go, but anger ran hot enough to jettison her away from his touch. By the time she spun to face him, hands on her hips, her temper had a mind of its own. "You're not any better than the Nameless Ones," she shouted. "They lied to me all the time too. If you're going after the Nameless Ones—or to rescue my friends—you have to take me. You need me. When you linked to me, you found the power to kill with your mind. Your men could do the same thing if we practiced.

"My friends will kill you before they let you get close enough to talk with them. They won't trust telepathic speech from you, either. You have to take me," she repeated. "There's no way around it."

Anger balled her hands into fists, and she drove one into a nearby wall, leaving a hole in the sheetrock.

Roy was on his feet in an instant and by her side. He pulled her into his arms, something she would have killed for a few minutes before, but now she writhed, hissing and spitting like a scalded cat. The bullets in his ammo belts cut into her.

"Let go of me."

"Never. Goddammit, Glory. I'm falling in love with you, and trying to do the right thing here. Does fraternization ring any bells?"

When he said *love*, it stopped her cold, and she quit fighting him. She ran *fraternization* through her brain and muttered, "To be friendly with someone. To spend time with someone in a friendly way, especially when it is considered wrong or improper to do so."

"Exactly."

"I don't get it. Why is you caring about me wrong?"

He gazed at her from his wonderfully blue eyes. "It's not, unless you're in a direct line of command under me."

What Roy had said about Uncle Miltie's words fell into a place where they made sense. "But you wouldn't put anyone else in danger to keep me safe."

A crooked smile lightened Roy's severe expression. "Oh, but I would. Including myself."

She dragged an arm upward and sifted her fingers through her shorn locks. "I can take care of myself. I've been well-trained. Have me report to Charlie or something."

Roy shook his head. "We work in small teams. It's the CIA way. I'm team leader."

"Then send a second team and assign me to that one."

The corners of Roy's mouth twitched into half a smile. "You're persistent."

"You bet I am." Glory laid the hand that she'd had in her hair on the back of his neck and dragged his mouth to hers. Maybe she took him by surprise, but he didn't turn away. The touch of his lips on hers drove everything else from her mind, and she clung to him, kissing him with a desperation borne of not having had him in her arms for days. He pushed his tongue into her mouth and his cock swelled against her belly.

Glory reached between them and pulled the sash to her robe open, wriggling it off her shoulders. Roy made a decidedly male sound, almost a growl, and ran kisses down her throat until he closed his mouth over her nipple, his teeth grazing sensitive flesh. She arched into him and closed her hand over his cock. It jumped in her hand, and she rubbed him through his pants, her breath coming fast as arousal raced through her.

He moved a hand between them and closed it over her mound, stroking her engorged nubbin. Between his mouth on her breast and his fingers rubbing her clit, a climax pounded through her, staggering in its intensity. It was the first time she'd come from something other than her own fingers. He kept rubbing and sucking, and she felt a second peak build.

Glory pushed into his mind. *"Feel me,"* she cried. *"Feel what you do to me."*

He didn't answer, but his cock grew longer and harder beneath her fingers. She fumbled the buttons of his pants open and he sprang into her hand, hot, rigid, and impossibly wonderful. She wanted to look at him, but she was so lost in lust, it was all she could do to remain upright. As her second climax spooled in her belly, she tightened her mind link with Roy, wanting him to share her ecstasy when she came.

Spasms ripped through her, and he exploded in her hand, jets of semen erupting as he repeated her name like a prayer, murmuring it around her nipple still in his mouth. He straightened and gathered her close, and his heart thudded beneath her ear.

"Didn't mean to do that," he said, working the words out in between panting gasps.

"I did. I've brought myself off every single night since I've been here thinking of you, hoping you'd come to me."

He kneaded her back and shoulders. "I was afraid if I did, I'd never leave." He let go long enough to scoop her robe off the floor. "Here, let me wipe up my mess."

She held her hands to him and felt his gaze skim her body. "God, Glory. You're so damned beautiful. I'll never get tired of looking at you," he said.

She shrugged the robe back over her shoulders, but let it hang open. "What if I feel the same way?"

His cell phone vibrated, and he stuffed his still hard cock back into his pants before drawing the phone out and glancing at the caller ID. He started to push ignore, but Glory grabbed the phone and tapped the answer icon before he could stop her.

"You're Milton Reins, right?" she said.

"And you must be Glory, which means Kincaid's not too far away." Uncle Miltie chuckled. "At least it explains why he's not on the helipad with the rest of his team. How'd you know it was me?" Mild curiosity underscored his words. "You can't have memorized our unique identifiers."

Glory sidestepped his question. "I want to talk with you. What time is good?"

After a pause that lasted so long, she was certain he'd tell her to go fuck herself, Uncle Miltie said, "Breakfast in half an hour in my office. Kincaid can show you where it is." The line went dead, and she handed the phone back.

Admiration etched into Roy's rugged face. "I have to hand it to you. You are one gutsy broad."

"I also reek of sex. I'm going to take a fast shower and get dressed. What should I wear? Field or dressy?"

"How did you know it was him? I'd like to know too." Roy bent to unlace his boots. "I'll join you in that shower, but no more sex or we'll be late. I'd love to tell you to wear a short skirt and high heels, but he'll take you more seriously if you dress like a commando."

"Got it." She trotted into the bathroom and flipped on the taps.

When he walked up behind her, she turned to him. "We haven't exactly had sex—except in my mind."

His smile melted her insides. "I'll remedy that as soon as I can, sweetheart." He brushed his lips over hers and swatted her rump. "Into the shower. Miltie's already pissed. We don't want to be late."

"You asked how I knew." She latched gazes with him. "I was still linked to your mind, and you recognized who was calling."

A look of grudging admiration started with his mouth and spread to his eyes. "Easy as that, huh?"

"Yup." She stepped over the rim of the tub. "Easy as that."

ROY LED AN UNNATURALLY quiet Glory to Uncle Miltie's office. The smell of bacon, eggs, and coffee hit him in the corridor before he even opened the door. Glory marched through—before Roy could announce them—and walked straight to Milton, who scrambled upright from his chair at a rectangular table pushed beneath a window. She held out her hand. "I'm Glory. Nice to meet you, sir."

"The pleasure's all mine." Milton's gaze shifted to Roy. "I can see why you're smitten, Kincaid, but we had a team ready to launch half an hour ago. I put them on hold until further notice."

"Sorry, sir. The teams already in the field need our support." Roy scanned Milton's office. Stacks of papers littered the floor next to a scarred, oak desk, with smaller piles dribbling to the table his boss used for meetings, strategy sessions, and today's breakfast. He cleared his throat. "I could have joined my men fifteen minutes ago, but you—"

"Never mind that," Milton buried Roy's words with his own. "The teams are holding their own right now, mostly dredging through wreckage for clues. Your men were actually backup—in case we ran into something unexpected." The CIA commander stared hard at Roy.

"Sorry, sir," Roy said again and held his boss's shrewd, dark-eyed gaze. Milton Reins had cut his teeth in the Vietnamese jungles by lying about his age and enlisting in the Marines when he was only fifteen. He'd clawed his way up the ranks, grabbing college degrees as they were offered, and had landed at the top of the CIA a year before he'd recruited Roy. As usual, Milton sported a tailored black business suit, white shirt, and blue tie. Shiny black loafers completed his outfit. His short black hair was shot with strands of silver. Even though he no longer went on field missions, he kept his body in peak condition with daily workouts that would have brought many younger men to their knees.

"The hell. You're not the least bit sorry." Uncle Miltie returned his attention to Glory. "Take a seat, young woman. Let me pour you some coffee. How do you like it?"

"Black, and I can get my own, sir."

"Nonsense. Sit down." His voice turned harsh. "That's an order."

Glory glanced at the table. It was obvious which seat Milton had staked out, so she selected one of the others. Roy shut the door, made his way to a chair, and settled into it. Milton slapped a cup in front of Glory and sat. "If you want coffee, Kincaid, you can get your own."

"What?" Roy quirked a brow. "The lady gets curbside service, and I don't?"

"Damn straight." Milton stuffed his napkin back in his lap, turned to Glory, and asked, "What do you want?"

She nodded. "I like you. You're direct."

Milton forked eggs into his mouth, chewed, and swallowed. "You still haven't told me what you want. I have a team ready to hit the field, young woman. Each hour they delay costs the taxpayers money. Also, how'd you know it was me on the phone? You never answered that question."

"Okay." She squared her shoulders. Roy noticed she hadn't touched her breakfast or coffee. "I knew because I saw who it was in Roy's mind." Milton opened his mouth, but Glory shook her head.

"That's not important. This is. You're making a mistake not letting Roy take me with him."

"Oh, really?" Silver brows lifted in surprise, and Roy bit back a laugh. It was probably years since anyone had told Uncle Miltie he'd made a mistake—at least to his face.

"Yes. The Nameless Ones—you call them freaks—trained me. I know how they think. Did Roy tell you how he linked with me and I taught him to kill, using just his mind?"

Milton's implacable gaze zeroed in on Roy, and he set his fork, loaded with eggs, down. "No. He left that niggling detail out."

Glory turned to stare at him too, with an incredulous look. "No wonder your boss said no," she told Roy. "You cherry-picked which bits of data to give him."

Roy held up a hand. "Okay." He glanced from Milton to Glory, before settling on Milton. "The injections created permanent alterations in my central nervous system. When Glory entered my mind, she showed me how to access things I wasn't aware of, and I was able to marshal the same power she uses. I've never tested it in the field—there hasn't been time."

"Damned gutsy of you to allow her access to your mind. Demonstration," Milton barked.

"Gladly." Glory got to her feet and walked to the far end of the large room. "What would you like him to use as a target?"

Roy joined her. "Maybe this isn't a good idea—" he started.

"Rubbish," Milton snapped. He strode to his desk, drew a slick-covered magazine from a drawer, and dropped it into a metal bowl. He placed the bowl on a metal stand and sat back down.

Roy moved the target to a corner of the office away from Milton and walked briskly back to their breakfast table. He glanced at Glory, who gave him a thumbs up. When he opened his mind, she slammed into it. Because they'd done this once before, it went fast. He extended his hands, power arced from them, and the magazine burst into flames.

The smoke detector squealed; Glory jabbed a finger at it, and it quieted.

"Impressive." Uncle Miltie stood, grabbed a fire extinguisher, and directed it at the blaze before opening a window. "Can you do it without her?"

"Yes, but I can't extend the power as far."

"He'll be able to," Glory broke in. "He just needs practice."

"Sit down and eat," Milton ordered. Once they were all back at the table, he asked, "Can my other men who've had the same drugs do this too?"

"Probably," Glory said, shoveling food into her mouth per instructions. Roy was proud of her, since she probably wasn't very hungry. He certainly wasn't.

She swallowed coffee and faced Uncle Miltie. "That's only one reason you need to include me. If part of your planned missions, either today or in the future, includes rescuing the women I lived with, they'll kill your men before they can get close. I have to be there because they trust me."

"Yeah, Kincaid touched on that part, but I disregarded it." Milton took more bacon from the serving dish and chewed thoughtfully. "What other little tricks do you have up your sleeve?"

Glory met his direct gaze. "To be honest, sir, I'm not exactly sure. The Nameless Ones weren't particularly forthcoming with us women. Beyond my enhanced physical and mental abilities and sharp senses, I can think things and have them happen. The only other skill I'm sure of is telepathic speech."

"How far can you project it?"

Roy smiled, since he'd asked the same question.

"Don't know that, either, sir. It hasn't been properly evaluated."

Milton scraped the remaining eggs off his plate. When he looked up, he nailed Roy with his dark eyes. "You didn't tell me everything because you were afraid I'd use her."

"Yes, sir."

"But she told me herself, so she's fair game."

"What exactly does that mean?" Glory cut in. Roy tried to shush her, but she just shot him an *I'm doing fine without you* look.

"What it means, young woman, is I expect you front and center in our underground practice area at zero nine hundred. That's one hour from now. Wear field gear, and plan to stay a while."

"Do you want the team there, sir?" Roy asked.

"Affirmative. I'll deploy a different backup team to the CDC."

"Will you be there too?"

A rare smile split Milton Reins' face. "Wouldn't miss it for the world, Kincaid. I'm particularly interested in how she turns her thoughts into reality."

CHAPTER 12

Glory plucked a towel from the rack and wiped sweat out of her eyes. They'd been locked down in the CIA's underground training facility for thirty-six hours. Uncle Miltie had seen to it that they had plenty of food, but he'd been clear no one was leaving until they'd determined the best way to leverage her abilities. None of the men had complained; neither had she. The facility was actually plush by her standards. Both men's and women's restrooms had showers, and bunks lined an adjacent room.

She dropped the towel and moved back to Charlie's side. "Want to try again?"

He nodded. "Sorry I lost it. I'm used to shielding myself when I feel those bastards poke into my head. Never does much good, so I end up killing as many as I can."

An idea blossomed. "What if I could show you how to ward your mind against them?"

The other six men trotted close. "We'd all like to learn that," Roy said.

She bit her lower lip, running possibilities through her data-processor brain. "Keep in mind, I've never tested this."

"Why not?" Milton asked from the corner of the room where he'd taken up residence.

"Because the Nameless Ones punished us for disobedience. They dropped us in solitary, and left us there for as much as a month on quarter rations."

Roy's face darkened. "Much more than a month and you'd have starved."

Bitterness surged. "That was the general idea. Some of the women did. The ones who were too thin to begin with."

Milton joined them. He patted her shoulder. "Nothing's quite as sweet as revenge. Link with Charlie and teach him how to keep your kinfolk out of his head." He scanned the group. "The rest of you listen up."

Glory extended a hand; Charlie clasped it and she pressed gently into his mind. Last time, she'd moved much faster and ended up on the ground, pinned under his weight, with the point of his knife at her throat, before Roy could pull him off. Hair trigger reactions were useful in the field, but it had taken all her self-control not to roast Charlie on the spot.

"Doing okay?" she asked. At his nod, she went. "Walk with me deeper into your mind. Notice where I open doors."

"I don't have doors in my head," he growled, his muscles tensing beneath her fingertips.

"Visualize them as passageways then." She kept her voice low, hypnotic. "Like this one." She nudged through a barrier in his mind. "And this one." She pushed another gateway open.

Charlie swallowed audibly. "How many are there?"

"Each person is different, but once we have six open, I'm going to give you something to do with them."

"Okay. I'm waiting." His brown eyes bored into her, and she sensed him treading the scruffy edge of sanity.

"There. Last one. Now, shut your eyes."

"Not on your life, sister."

"Okay," she agreed. "It's easier for me to visualize things with my eyes closed, but I'll trust you to do what works best for you. Dig into the first place we opened and draw out something that looks kind of like cobwebby material." She waited until he gave a terse nod, his eyes still wide and staring. "Now do that with the other five gateways. Once you have the stuff in hand, twist it together."

"Doesn't want to go." He gritted his teeth, and a muscle jumped high on one cheek.

"You're trying too hard. Relax. Close your eyes." She moved through his mind, gathering the protective sheathing he'd unearthed so it was all in one place. Glory waited. He could do this, but he had to believe in himself—and in her. The blobs of sticky fibers moved closer to each other.

"Yes," she encouraged. "Keep doing exactly what you're doing, and then visualize them twisting, joining."

A loud clack bounced her from his mind. Glory grinned. "See. You did it. You pushed me out, and I'll bet I can't get back in. Not while you have those wards deployed."

Charlie opened his eyes, and swiped the back of one hand over his sweating forehead. "Christ almighty. How can I do anything else and this too? It took all my concentration."

"Only because it was something brand new," she said. "Like everything, it gets easier with practice." She looked around the group. "Did any of the rest of you do that along with us?" Everyone nodded. "Great!" She flexed her fingers, cracking her knuckles. "Get those shields up, men, and let's see if I can pop them. Once you've got this part down, I'll show you how to augment your warding to not only keep the Nameless ones out of your head, but also hide your presence from them."

Roy met her gaze. "If you could hide your presence, how'd they find you?"

"It takes a lot of energy to keep shielding up all the time. I had to sleep, and I wasn't as efficient when I was cold and hungry."

"Never again." Roy's words brushed her mind. *"Not cold. Not hungry. Not on my watch."*

Glory felt her face heat and dipped her head so the others wouldn't see. She clapped her hands smartly. "Shields up. You have thirty seconds and I'll try to beat my way through them."

~

Hours passed. Glory should have been tired, but she wasn't. Teaching the men, and expanding the edges of what she knew about her own skills, held a heady aspect. For the first time in her life, she felt useful, and she reveled in it. No longer a second class citizen, fighting for basic rights like a place to sleep and food in her belly, she'd moved to being a valued team member. She blessed Roy for taking a chance on her that night in the café. Without his help, she'd probably be right back at the compound sitting in a punishment cell.

Or dead.

He caught her eye from across the room and winked. Who knew? Maybe he'd divined her thoughts. They'd all gotten better at poking into one another's heads.

She was grateful to Milton too. He could have blown her off this morning, ordered Roy to join his team, and then none of this would have happened. The only skill where she'd run into a snag was thinking things into being. She'd been able to do simple things like move objects from the next room and turn things off and on, but she hadn't managed to create something that wasn't already there. Maybe she needed practice, or maybe there was a trick she didn't know about to coax that talent into full bloom.

Something more pressing bothered her, though. One of the men didn't feel quite right. He held her at the barest edges of his mind, no matter how much she encouraged him. Yet he was able to perform defensive moves, deploying the power of his mind to send killing blows into dummies, while they fought on something like a holodeck from Star Trek reruns she'd watched on the Internet.

She needed to have a private conversation with Roy, but wasn't certain how to finesse it. "Dinner," Milton shouted. "Thirty minutes, then it's back at it. I want to determine how far you can project telepathic communication next."

"What happens after that, boss?" Roy asked.

Uncle Miltie grinned. "You map out a fresh plan of attack and get your asses out of here. By my count, this mission is days late."

"You got it, sir." Roy snapped a salute in Uncle Miltie's direction.

"Stand down," Milton growled. "This isn't the damned Army."

"Does that mean I'm included?" Glory tilted her chin defiantly and stared at Milton.

He made a sound midway between a snort and a grunt. "You've made yourself indispensable. You're part of the team. Get used to it." He narrowed his eyes. "I'll have personnel get your paperwork together while you're gone. You can sign your life away next time I see you."

Glory moved to Roy's side. *"I need to talk with you."* She shielded her speech, but wasn't certain how much good it would do now that all the men were fine tuning abilities unlocked by the injections they'd taken.

He sent a shrewd glance her way and made a come along gesture with one hand. She followed him up onto the holodeck and back to its control panel. He tapped a few buttons, and a flickering screen dropped between them and the rest of the room. "Should be safe enough," he said, "since that thing throws out white noise. Talk fast."

"That man, John Rollins. How long have you worked with him?"

"I haven't. Milton hired him after I went undercover hunting for the scientists. He replaced Ted, a man killed during the team's last mission."

"There's something wrong with him," she said flatly. "He doesn't feel right to me."

Roy thinned his lips into a harsh line. "All right. This is probably stickier than checking his records. If he infiltrated us, his creds had to be impeccable."

"We can't take him with us," Glory insisted. The more she thought about it, the less she trusted him.

"Okay. We can't stay back here any longer. It'll look suspicious—and set him off if he's not what he says." Roy reversed the knobs and buttons, and the screen dispersed. "Come on, sweetheart." He gave her an obvious peck on the cheek, probably so the others would think they'd snuck a private moment to cuddle. "Let's hit the chow line."

"You're funny." She leaned into him, and together they walked briskly to plates of sandwiches, small tubs of macaroni and potato salad, and warm cookies. Milton raised his eyebrows in a silent question, but Roy shook his head. They helped themselves to dinner and found seats. Before they finished, Milton joined them.

"I was considering sending everyone back to their quarters after this next exercise," he said.

"Not a good idea. I want everyone here until we're ready to pull out," Roy replied.

"Any particular reason?"

"Not one I'm willing to share."

Uncle Miltie frowned and shot to his feet, crooking a finger at Roy. "Come with me."

Roy sent an encouraging look her way and followed his boss out of the room.

Glory returned her attention to her dinner. The corned beef sandwich had been delectable, with fatty meat that melted in her mouth. Maybe she'd finally manage to gain a little weight here in the land of plenty.

Charlie dropped into the chair Roy had vacated. "I just wanted to thank you," he said. "And apologize again for squashing you." He rolled his eyes. "After as long as I've been at this, defensive moves are automatic."

"It's okay." She looked down, not wanting to admit how close she'd come to taking him out because her own defensive moves were automatic too.

"Where'd my two bosses go?"

"I have no idea." She spooned the last of the potato salad into her mouth. "Why?"

"Our half hour break's up. Maybe we could practice while we wait for Roy to come back."

"Why not?" She got to her feet and loped to the drinking fountain to wash down her supper. Once she wasn't thirsty anymore, she rejoined Charlie. "Want to start testing the limits of telepathic speech?"

"It was the next task, according to Uncle Miltie—"

"Does he know you all call him that?" she broke in.

Charlie grinned. It softened the harsh planes of his face. "He'd almost have to. Come on. I'll rally the troops."

They began with only a few feet between communication pairs. She listened in, checking on each, and then they moved ten feet farther away. Time dribbled by. Where was Roy? The men had moved to the extreme opposite ends of the large room, and were still able to communicate with ease. What they needed was for some of them to move outside, preferably at quarter mile, half mile, and mile markers.

She was about to suggest they'd done all they could without permission to leave the practice area when Roy and Milton trotted back into the room. She filled them in on what she and Charlie had done.

"Excellent." Roy clapped her on the back. "Well played. You and Charlie will go to the munitions building next. It's close to a mile away. Once you're there, we'll try to talk. If that works, Charlie will come back here, and I'll send the other men to you one at a time, since they all need to experiment with turning their thoughts into long-range speech. If it doesn't, we'll have you move closer."

Glory picked something up beneath his cheerful orders. She narrowed her eyes in silent question, but he shook his head ever so slightly. He had something in mind, but what? She tried to push into his head and smothered a smile when she realized he was shielding his thoughts just like she'd taught him.

Charlie tossed a jacket her way, and she caught it on the fly. "Cold out there," he said.

She slipped into the fleece with a CIA logo on it and zipped up, pulling the hood over her head. "Ready." She caught Charlie's eye. "You'll have to show me where the munitions building is."

"Feel like a jog?"

She did. They'd been stuck in the practice room for far too long. "You're on. Race you."

~

Roy watched Glory lope out of the room with Charlie, wishing he'd had a chance to clue his trusted teammate in on his concerns.

Per the plan he and Milton had just hatched, Uncle Miltie moved to where the rest of the team milled about and mapped out elements of what would be expected of them for the telepathy exercise. Once he was done with that, he involved them in brainstorming how to implement their new talents. While the team's attention was on his boss, Roy slipped out of the room and made his way to a vantage point close to the munitions building.

He used the trick Glory taught them to mask both his thoughts and his presence from anyone who might have the ability to sense his energy field. Charlie and Glory stood for a while, seeing if they could talk with those back in the underground room. When it was clear they could, Charlie left, saying he'd send the next man her way.

Glory paced in a small circle. He worried she might be cold, but her eyes shone with enthusiasm. He wanted to go to her, tell her he'd laid a trap for John, but he needed her mind to be clean. If John wasn't what he appeared, who knew what he could do? Roy loosened his Sig in its holster and clicked off the safety.

Glory's head popped up, and he kicked himself for not

remembering her extraordinarily sharp hearing. Fortunately, John sprinted into view and made his way to Glory's side. His appearance gave her something to link the unexpected noise to.

She smiled and asked, "Ready? It worked fine for Charlie."

John glanced about and narrowed his eyes.

Roy's gut tensed, and he readied himself for damn near anything. He'd picked the munitions building because it was deserted at this hour, as was the campus surrounding it. He judged the distance between him and John.

"Come on," Glory urged. "It's cold out here, and I've got four more guys after you, plus Roy."

John swung to face her. "You little bitch," he spat. "Thought you could get away with selling us out, did you?"

Her body jerked, spine arching backward, and she twisted from side to side, snared in something Roy couldn't see. John must have bound her somehow. What would happen to her if he shot the man? John's death should release any sort of hold he had on Glory, but Roy wasn't totally certain.

"What are you going to do?" she ground out. "If you kill me, they'll be onto you."

"I have no intention of killing you," he retorted. "If I did that, the other women would make a martyr out of you, an urban legend. We have other plans. Can't let you run off and not make an example of your insubordination. I've got people inside with me. Once you're back at your compound, they'll cover my tracks. I'll have to disappear, but the others will still be here."

"Why didn't I sense you before?" Glory writhed against invisible bonds.

A nasty smile split John's face. "Because I'm V4. You didn't think we'd stop with your flawed model, did you?"

The muted chop of rotor blades scraped Roy's hearing. No one would think twice about a chopper over Langley, which was likely what the Nameless Ones counted on. The bird could be on the ground and gone in under five minutes.

Roy had heard enough. Long years as an operative had taught him to make quick decisions and sort out the pieces later. He raised the Sig in a fluid motion and sent a single bullet into the side of John's head. It was a hollow point, designed to wreak maximum havoc by forging an ever-widening path inside the body.

A surprised look washed over the man's face. Roy bolted from his hiding place and shot him again at point blank range, pumping bullets into him until he crumpled to the ground. It was overkill, but what the hell.

"You all right?" He shot a worried glance at Glory.

"Fine. His hold on me shattered after your first bullet." She shook herself. "Thanks. I should have warded myself, but I wasn't totally certain he was one of *them*, and it never occurred to me he'd try something in the middle of Langley."

Roy strode to her side and keyed his mic. "Boss?"

"Right here."

"There's a chopper about two hundred fifty feet above the munitions building that seems to be leaving. Suggest defensive measures."

"You got it. Casualties?"

"One. Send the cleanup crew."

"Tell Glory it was a good call on her part."

Roy grinned. "I will, sir." He turned to Glory. "Did you hear that?"

"Of course." She scrubbed her hands down her face. "You didn't tell Uncle Miltie there are other Nameless Ones here."

Roy kissed her forehead, deeply grateful she was still alive. If the freaks hadn't been so bent on retribution—and Glory hadn't sensed danger—John would have killed her and escaped in the helicopter. "I will, just as soon as we get back. This external channel's not totally secure—especially not now." He draped an arm around her shoulders. "Come on. Let's get you back inside."

"What about the other men and communications practice?"

"If it worked for Charlie at a mile, it will work for them. The next exercise is determining the outer limits of that ability, and we won't be doing that tonight."

He started walking, gun still clasped in the hand that wasn't around her body. "How're you doing?"

She shook her head. "I don't know. When it was looking as if that bastard was going to shanghai me and whisk me back to the compound, all I could think about was losing you." She bit her lower lip. "Stupid of me. I should have been figuring out how to defeat the noose he snared me with."

"Would there have been a way to keep him from trapping you in the first place?"

"I think so, but like I said, it never occurred to me I had to be on the defensive in here." She inhaled a shuddery breath, stopped walking, and turned to face him. "This will never be over, will it? They'll never leave me alone." Her eyes filled with tears, but she blinked them away.

"It will be over," he promised. "I won't quit until we've taken down every single one of those motherfuckers."

"Unless they get you first," she muttered. "Ach, Christ! I didn't mean I don't believe in you, but they're sly. Look how they finessed tonight. John must have been communicating with other Nameless Ones, otherwise they wouldn't have had a helicopter so close." Her eyes widened. "Wait a minute," she said. "There's our answer about how far telepathic communication extends."

He snorted. "Indeed. Pretty fucking far. Come on. It's cold out here."

They resumed walked toward the underground practice facility. "Until we determine who the other Nameless Ones are, we'll have to be extremely careful about disclosing plans for anything," he said, and made a disgusted noise. "No wonder so many of our missions blew up in our face. They knew we were coming."

"No shit. How about the rest of your team? Do you trust them?" Worry drove a furrow between her eyes.

"They're fine. They've all been with The Company since before the rebellion."

A relieved sigh burbled past her lips. "Thank God."

He placed his palm on a glass plate to release the locking mechanism and held the door to the practice facility open for her.

"*N*o, goddammit!" Roy pounded his fist on the round table in a shielded room deep beneath CIA headquarters.

Glory turned to stare at him, and Milton Reins burst out laughing. "Never would have pegged you for the Neanderthal type, Kincaid."

Roy shoved his shoulders straight and rotated his neck to ease the tension that had turned his muscles into rocks. It didn't help much. The three of them had relocated to this claustrophobic space with brown walls, brown chairs, and a brown table after he and Glory returned to the practice area. Milton had sent the other men back to base side quarters.

Things were going well enough at the CDC and Johns Hopkins attack sites that Milton agreed to deploy Roy's team to Washington State. They'd been kicking around the fine points of springing the women from Glory's dorm at the compound for over an hour. Roy wasn't used to being challenged, and his frustration level shot through the roof.

"You're not listening," he told Glory. "Authorizing you to undertake a solo mission isn't in anybody's interest."

"You're the one who's not listening," she countered. "It's not a solo mission. You and the team will be close by. It's the simplest, cleanest way to get the women out. Besides, I need you to provide a diversion so I can get inside. If you come with me, the women won't listen, they'll react. They'll never believe you're not holding me hostage." She stood and walked to a whiteboard where she picked up a red marker and began sketching something. When she was done, a horizontal line bisected by two vertical ones at its ends mocked him.

"This," she pointed and drew a triangle, "is the main door. Usually, it's the only way inside, and a guard is always posted."

"What makes you think you can go through a window without activating an alarm?" Roy asked.

"One didn't go off when I left," she pointed out. "At least nothing audible. I suppose they could've installed an alarm system in a couple weeks, but I doubt it. Their senses are so keen, they'd never believe they needed one.

"We'll do this late at night," she went on. "Maybe two a.m. You and the team will storm the man guarding the front door. All the Nameless Ones will rush there. While they're busy, I open a window, slide through, rustle up the girls, and retrace my steps."

"Are you certain they'll come with you?" Milton asked.

"Yes, of course. Why would you even ask?"

Roy had known Milton a long time, so he understood his boss's expression meant he was sugarcoating his words. "Even if you and the women fantasized about running away, most of them will be too paralyzed to act on it."

Glory frowned, opened her mouth, and then closed it again. She made her way back to the table and sat. "I see what you're getting at, but I can't imagine them not wanting out of there."

"It may be hell," Roy said quietly, "but it's their hell."

Understanding shone from her eyes, green again since there was no longer a need to shield her identity. "I get it." She dropped her gaze and studied her hands. "Maybe it's a fool's errand, but I have to try. I can't just leave them there."

"You won't have time for discussion," Roy said. "They're either behind you heading for the open window, or not."

"I understand."

"Do you?" Milton turned the full power of his dark eyes on Glory. "These are women you shared living quarters with for seven years. Maybe even before that if you could remember. They're the closest thing you have to family. You're going to have to leave the ones who don't jump on your offer. And the ones you leave behind will die when the place blows."

Roy watched her throat work as she swallowed. "I won't put myself at risk any more than I have to," she said.

"Are you certain you can't reach them telepathically and lead them to the window that way?" Roy asked.

She blew out a tired sounding breath. "We've been over that ground. There's no way I can send any sort of telepathic message and not have the Nameless Ones pick it up."

"You'll have fifteen minutes," Milton said.

"You and whoever leaves with you has to be clear by then," Roy added.

"I get it." She balled both hands into fists and shook them in the air in front of her before opening her hands and flexing her fingers. "You're blowing the place up. If I'm still inside, I'll die."

Roy opened his mouth, but before he could get any words out, Milton said, "We're good here. Nothing to say that hasn't already been said. Grab a few hours' sleep before you drive to the rendezvous point. You leave at zero six hundred."

"Vehicle?" Roy snapped out.

"I'll text you where to pick it up."

"Understood." Roy got to his feet and motioned to Glory, who did the same.

"About the other Nameless Ones here—" she began.

"In process," Milton said. "Get some sleep. I have a feeling you'll need it."

"So we're driving to where a jet will pick us up?" Glory asked.

Roy nodded. "No talking about this, or even thinking about it, once we leave this room."

"They already know where I am," she said. "They can track my energy. I'll have to be extra careful to shield it."

"They probably won't expect you'd head back into their clutches," Roy pointed out. "It should offer an element of surprise."

"I hope so."

Milton made shooing motions with both hands. "The two of you are harder to get rid of than a stray dog."

Roy tipped his head so the door's retinal scanner could verify his identity before the lock disengaged. He walked through with Glory right at his heels, and then waited until she was next to him so he could slip an arm through hers. "Nervous?" he asked as they made their way toward the elevator that would carry them two hundred feet up to ground level.

"That's one word for it. Petrified is another. Shit! I was scared when I stole that data, and the odds here are much more daunting."

"It's good you recognize it," he said. "Never underestimate your enemies."

"Did someone famous say that?"

Roy chuckled. "Not exactly. Someone did say never interrupt your opponent when they're in the midst of making a mistake."

She glanced at him and smiled. It lightened what had been an edgy mood. "Walk me to my room?"

"I was hoping for something more than leaving you at your door."

A blush swooshed up her throat and splotched color across her cheeks, and she leaned into him. "Me too."

"How about this?" he murmured. "For tonight, we just enjoy each other. No yesterdays. No tomorrows." He laid his palm on an electronic pad next to the elevator to call the car. Silver doors whooshed open, and he motioned her inside in front of him.

Glory took his hand, twining her fingers with his. "I can do that. Pft," she scoffed. "My whole life was make believe—and it still feels that way. If I'd let myself think of years rolling forward, dancing to their tune, I'd have hung myself."

His heart stuttered against his chest. "I'm very glad you didn't."

"Some of the women did. Not in my dorm, but we heard rumors."

"Uh-uh." He faced her and laid a hand over her mouth. "No yesterdays."

"And no tomorrows." She pressed her lips together.

The elevator doors opened. They walked through and made their way to her apartment building. Her scent eddied about him in the cold, damp air. She clung to his hand like a lifeline. If it were up to him, he'd keep her here at Langley under twenty-four hour guard, so long as each of those guards was thoroughly vetted.

She fitted her chin so the retinal scanner could read her eye, and they entered her secure building. Roy nodded to the agent standing in the lobby. He'd known the man for as long as he'd been with the CIA, so chances of him being a Nameless One were nil.

As they walked down the second floor hallway to her rooms, she said, "You can't keep me in a box."

He stood aside while she opened her door and followed her inside. "You were in my head, huh?"

Glory pulled her jacket off and hung it over a hook next to the front door. He followed suit. She faced him and tapped his chest with an index finger. "No yesterdays or tomorrows for you, either."

Feelings for the woman standing before him threatened to choke him. "It's only fair." He slid his hands beneath her hair. "Let me draw us a bath."

The corners of her mouth twitched. "Guess that's a backhanded way of saying we both stink."

He shrugged. "We were in the underground practice facility for

the better part of two days. I always like to wash that place off me."
He rubbed his thumb over her full lips. "I want this to be as perfect
as it can be for you. Let me fuss over you tonight."

She arched her brows. "The closest anyone's ever come to
fussing over me was when you cut and colored my hair." She shot
him a shy smile. "A girl could get used to being fawned over."

Roy dragged her against him, reveling in the press of her tall,
curvy form. He wanted to hold her, protect her, build a shrine to
her. He cradled her head between his hands and murmured
wordless endearments. Before he kissed her and things got out of
hand, he moved back enough to lead her to a chair. Once she sat, he
knelt and unlaced her boots, jockeying them off one by one. She
made pleased, little noises at his touch and arched her feet into
his hands.

"I'll get the bath running," he said. "Don't move. I'll be
right back."

By the time he adjusted the temperature and found scented bath
salts in one of the bathroom cabinets, she appeared stark naked in
the bathroom doorway. He grinned, unable to look away from the
wonder of her body. Tall, slender, but with bands of shapely muscle
on shoulders, arms, and legs, she was truly a work of art. Her
breasts sat high atop a sculpted ribcage with dark brown, puckered
nipples. Her stomach was concave, and a curly black mat covered
her pussy.

"Thought I told you not to move."

"Sometimes I don't follow directions very well."

The words sent up an alarm, and he wanted to launch into a
lecture about how her life would depend on her following
directions, but they'd made a pact. No yesterdays. No tomorrows.
The unspoken warning left a bitter taste he swallowed down.

Glory tucked her fingers under the edge of his top and tugged it
over his head. She looked at the straps holding his Kevlar vest in
place, figuring them out and untwining them. "Will I have one
of these?"

He nodded. "It will be in the jet that picks us up, along with field gear for the team. I signed you up for weapons practice this last week. Did you learn enough to shoot a gun?"

He made a grab for her wrists. "Don't answer that. I do not want work to intrude. Not tonight. Tonight is ours."

"It's tough." She raised her green eyes to meet his. "Shutting out the world."

"Nothing harder." Roy forced himself to hold her gaze. It had been so difficult for him, he'd gone overboard the other way. All work. Nothing else. Not since Lorna's death. He didn't count the occasional bout of nameless, faceless sex. In some ways, that had felt like work too. Sometimes he needed empty balls for a clear head.

He shrugged out of his bulletproof vest, and she pulled his undershirt off, tracing the line of his nipples with a fingertip. Sensation shot straight to his groin.

"Your boots." She glanced at his feet.

He sat on the floor and worked his feet out of his high-top, thick-soled boots while she turned off the water before the tub overflowed.

"Are you going to stand up?" She smiled down at him, looking like an angel.

He pushed upright, and she reached for the waistband of his pants. He stood quietly while she undid his trousers and pushed them down his legs, followed by his shorts. His cock was hard, standing out from a jungle of coppery hair between his legs.

Glory ran her hand up his shaft, examining it intently. His legs shook from wanting her, and he said, "Into the tub, you little vixen. I want to get to the next part, and if you keep stroking me, we'll never get clean."

"Vixen," she murmured. "A female fox, or a woman who nags or criticizes." She glared at him, and said, "I do not."

He scooped her into his arms and climbed over the rim of the tub, holding her wriggling body tight against him. With her still squirming and giggling, he lowered them both into the steaming water and plucked a cloth off a nearby rack. When she was cradled between his legs, leaning against his chest, he said, "The dictionary definitions often miss idiomatic meaning. Vixen can also mean a tease, and if restraining myself from not ravishing your amazing nakedness isn't you teasing me, I don't know what is."

He rubbed a bar of lavender scented soap over her belly and breasts and sluiced water over her with the washcloth. She twisted, kneeling before him and washed him, so close the tips of her breasts brushed against his chest.

"You already washed my dick." He laughed, loving the feel of her hands on him.

"Did I, now?" She gazed at him, eyes full of coquettish innocence. "I must have forgotten."

He slipped his hand between her legs and she made a little mewling noise and ground her pubes against his palm. "We're clean enough, Glory," he said, his voice rougher than he'd meant, but he wanted her so much desire filled every cell, every nerve with sweet longing.

She flowed to her feet and stepped out of the tub. Her creamy skin was blotched with wanting him. He pulled the drain plug, stood, and was by her side an instant later, wrapping a towel around her and blotting himself with another, but he didn't care about being dry. What he wanted was Glory in his arms, up close and personal.

He placed his hands on her shoulders, turned her to face him, and gazed at her for long moments before he pulled her close, towel and all. She angled her head, and he slashed his mouth over hers, not able to get enough of her luscious lips and questing tongue. She hooked her arms beneath his and splayed her hands over his shoulder blades, raking him with her short nails.

His cock jerked where it was trapped between their bodies. The heat of her and the rough pressure of the terrycloth towel were almost enough to make him lose control. He ripped his mouth from hers, scooped her into his arms and walked them to the bed.

"No one's carried me since I was a child," she said, breathless and laughing. "Not that I remember anything about my childhood, but someone would've had to carry me before I could walk."

"Are you complaining?" He laid her gently atop the bed and knelt over her, running kisses down her neck to her breasts. She didn't answer, just bowed her back into his touch. He suckled first one nipple, then the other, as she writhed beneath him with her fingers tangled in his hair.

Glory, a stunning, rosy-faced Glory, pulled his head away from her breasts. "Was I hurting you?" he asked, searching her face for clues.

She shook her head. "Lie down. I want to look at you." A wanton grin made her look young, carefree. "This is my first experience with a living, breathing model. I want to take full advantage of it."

Roy kissed his way back to her mouth and lay on his side, facing her. He stroked her face, her breasts, her side, her back, while she explored him with eyes and fingers, lingering over his achingly hard cock.

"You're beautiful," she murmured. "So beautiful."

The words should have made him uncomfortable. Instead, joy cut deep. He wanted to be everything to her, fill her every need. She kissed him deeply, thrusting her tongue inside his mouth, before licking her way down to his nipples. His cock jerked alarmingly, and he clamped down on his lust. This was her first time; everything had to be for her. Because he didn't want it to get in the way later, he twisted away long enough to grab the condom packet he'd left next to the bed and slip the thin sheath over himself.

When her mouth tracked lower on his chest and he divined her intent, he gripped her head between his hands. "No, sweetheart. If you do that, I'll come. I'm perilously close as it is."

"But I want to bring you pleasure."

He drew her back beside him, and turned her onto her back. "Just looking at you, having you in my arms, brings me pleasure. You're a virgin. Let me make this as easy as I can." He swirled his fingers around her passion-slick nub until it swelled and stiffened. Then he pushed a finger inside her hot tightness, leaving his palm pressed against her clit. She bucked her hips upward, trying to draw him deeper, and cried out as an orgasm shook her.

Roy rode it through until her spasms subsided, and then knelt over her and wrapped a hand around his cock to guide himself inside. "Put your legs around me." It was all he could do to get the words out, he wanted her so much.

Her intense gaze never left him while she wound her legs around his hips and scooted closer. Her nipples were tight buds of desire, and her chest blushed with color from her climax. He seated himself at the entrance to her body, pushed inside a little, and then stopped. He felt her brush against his mind, as she rotated her hips to encourage him to move deeper.

"What are you doing?"

"I want to feel everything the same way you do," she panted. "Every single thing. You can do the same. Join with me. All the way. Nothing held back."

Roy pooled his consciousness with hers and moved into an altered reality. He felt his cock inside her at the same time as he felt her pussy around him. The dual layers of feedback were incredibly erotic, as he sank inside her waiting body. He felt her discomfort when he pushed past her hymen and waited until desire outstripped pain before continuing.

Even though it was killing him, he forced long slow strokes until her next climax bloomed deep in her belly. He felt it spool, build, and shatter her with its release. He moved his hips faster, seeking his own peak. It was there, so close. Deep in his head, Glory urged him on, tightened her muscles around him, and milked his shaft until semen boiled from him in hot, viscous spurts.

Roy came for a long time, shaken by the intensity of the strongest orgasm of his life. She pulled him into her arms, and he lay atop her gasping and panting as his heart rate normalized. He was still in her mind, and she was still in his.

He shifted to his side and pulled her into his arms, cock still buried inside her body. "I'm in love with you, sweetheart." He stroked her hair and gazed into her amazing eyes.

"Me too," she murmured, "but reversed." Glory smiled. "That didn't come out quite right."

"Never mind, I understood. Sleep, darling. Morning will be here much too soon."

She settled against him and drifted off almost immediately. Roy wasn't able to take his own advice. As he cradled her, fear battered him. Tomorrow would be logistics and travel, but the night after, they'd attack. Would this be the only time he'd ever have with Glory? Nothing in his business was certain. It was why he'd ignored female agents, considering hooking up with tantamount to courting disaster.

Too late. The die is cast. I'll do my God damnedest to protect her.

His cock slid from her body and he reached to retrieve the condom, careful not to disturb the woman slumbering in his arms.

CHAPTER 14

Glory fidgeted, searching for a more comfortable position in her hard, flat seat on the plane that had rendezvoused with the team at Bolling Air Force Base. The military jet was sleek and fast, but shy on comfort. The flight gave her time to think, and her first revelation stunned her. The intensity and delight of lovemaking with Roy explained why she and the other women had been off limits to the Nameless Ones. When men were sunk in rut, they couldn't possibly keep their minds shielded, so anything they knew turned into fair game for any woman close enough to look.

What a lost opportunity. If she'd understood the potential power, she'd have taken advantage of it. Maybe then, she'd know about where she came from, and have a better understanding of how the Nameless Ones had organized after the rebellion.

If I'd done that, what Roy and I did last night wouldn't feel so special.

Warmth from sharing his body still suffused her. They'd made love again in the middle of the night, this time with her straddling him. Just thinking about his hard-muscled body started a slow heat in her belly that spread downward. Maybe once this mission was over, they could sneak away for a day and fuck each other blind. She smiled at the thought.

Her mind was restless, filled with Roy's Adonis body and his long, thick cock. To divert herself, she stretched her consciousness toward the jet's computer system, joining with it effortlessly. For a time, she monitored the complexity that kept the craft in the sky, marveling at the engineering acumen that maintained each system in sync with the others. She'd merged with simple artificial intelligence before, but nothing this multifaceted, except maybe the helicopter that had picked them up near Madison. Once she understood the plane well enough to both fly it and construct another—at least on paper—she withdrew, cautious not to get in the way of anything.

An idea took form, and she ran it through her high tech brain, looking for flaws. Excitement filled her as she fine-tuned what she hoped would become a foolproof solution once they got to the compound.

Roy dropped into the seat beside her. "We'll be landing at McChord Air Force Base in about half an hour. We'll stay there tonight, going over last minute plans. Tomorrow at noon, we'll move out and get into position, scope out our target. We strike at midnight."

She wanted to tell him her idea, but didn't. If no one knew but her, and the women she aimed to rescue, it would up the odds that she'd succeed. "Thanks," she murmured. "It will be good to get this over with."

He leaned close, mouth near her ear so his breath tickled her. "Once this is done, I made reservations at a little bed and breakfast in the San Juan Islands. Just you and me, sweetheart, for an entire day, and two nights. We'll catch a commercial flight back to Langley afterward."

Her heart did a funny little flip flop, and she felt her face heat, deeply pleased he cared enough to plan something special just for them. "I can hardly wait."

He covered her hand with his briefly, and then stood. "I'll be in the cockpit until we land."

"The pilot's a friend of yours, isn't he?"

Roy grinned down at her. "Guess we'll never have any secrets. He used to work for me. He's a good man. We've been catching up."

As she watched Roy stride down the aisle, Glory double checked the shielding in her mind. Not having secrets was fine and well, but she was certain Roy wouldn't approve of her latest brainchild. Since it wouldn't put anyone but her in the line of fire, she didn't see any reason to tell him and create an argument. They could hash it out later, and she'd give her word to never do anything like this again—ever.

GLORY, Roy, and Charlie hunkered in a shadowed glade a mile from the compound. Greasepaint blacked their faces, and they were dressed in black from head to toe. She'd covered her newly-blonde locks with a watch cap. It was a good thing she'd left the compound on foot, otherwise it would have been difficult to find again. The mountainous, dirt roads were narrow and winding with interminable side roads branching in all directions. The Nameless Ones utilized a variant of the chaff they shielded themselves with to mask the compound from electronic surveillance and prying eyes.

The night felt damp and cold, the temperature hovering just below freezing. Ice crystals glittered on standing pools of water and on leafless bushes and trees. A quarter moon alternately flickered and hid as clouds passed over it. The strident cry of a hunting hawk reached her ears, followed by frantic squeaks from the rodent it had targeted.

Her breath plumed in the air, and she rubbed her hands together before stuffing them into her jacket pockets to keep them warm. The other four men were getting into position, and they'd launch soon.

"Go ahead." Charlie's voice was gruff. "Say your goodbyes, we need to hit it."

Roy gave her a quick hug. "I altered protocol. You heard at the briefing. From the stroke of midnight, you'll have twenty minutes. Make the most of them. Once you're down to less than five, make for your exit, no matter what."

Glory hugged him back. "I understand." She wanted to cling to him, never leave the shelter of his arms, but she forced herself to step back. "Charlie's right. We need to move."

They crept through thick, ice-coated underbrush single file with Roy first, her next, and Charlie bringing up the rear. Glory threw her augmented senses wide open. Of all of them, she'd had by far the most practice. They had field mics in addition to the ability to communicate telepathically. She thought the mics might be less likely to be detected, but she wasn't certain. Bottom line was they were only to communicate if absolutely necessary. Roy's words ran through her mind.

Follow the plan. Only open a channel if you've been captured and need backup to spring you.

The compound came into view. It wouldn't have been visible without her enhanced night vision. She tapped Roy's back, nodded sharply after he turned to glance at her, and took off on a diagonal, moving from shadow to shadow as she drew closer to her target. Uneasiness flowed from him in waves. She wanted to tell him not to worry, but couldn't, so she kept moving. Action quelled the knot in her belly and the tightness balled at the back of her throat.

Would the women want to leave? Or was Uncle Miltie right about them being probable Stockholm Syndrome victims?

Can't worry about that now. Even if I don't leave with them, hopefully I can merge with the master computer here and drain its databanks.

She reached the compound's outer wall and moved silently beneath the set of windows closest to where her dormitory was. She was a few minutes early, but that was all to the good. Marshaling a short burst of kinetic energy, she popped the window a foot above her head and waited, not daring to breathe. It should lead to a storage room, unless someone had moved into it since she left.

Her heart slammed against her ribcage and sweat slicked her sides. Once she'd counted to fifty without sensing anyone's energy closing to investigate the open window, she curved her fingers over the sill and clambered over it. It was farther to the floor than she expected, still a two foot drop even after she hung from her hands on the inside of the building. She bent her knees to absorb the shock and let herself fall.

So far. So good. She stayed in a crouch, every sense alight with the adrenaline coursing through her, but no one shot through the closed door intent on doing away with her. Understanding raced into her brain. The master computer hadn't set off an alarm because it recognized her energy signature. Apparently, the Nameless Ones hadn't bothered to scrub her from its memory.

Glory tamped down her jubilation. This might be easier than she'd hoped. She sent a silent prayer Roy's way and wished him smooth sailing before she unlocked the deadbolt and scanned the hall.

Empty.

She borrowed the Nameless One's trick and sent power to rotate the electronic eyes lining the wall so they faced the ceiling. A deep breath, and one more, and she flew down the fifty feet of hall separating her from the dorm she'd once called home. Hoping the Nameless One's sloppiness extended to the electronic scanners, she placed her palm over the glass plate by the door. The slight snick of the lock thrilled her, and she pushed the door open.

Moving fast, she started with Charity. "Leave with me."

"What?" the other woman asked sleepily. "How?"

"What are you doing back here?" Faith called from her bed, her voice muted.

"Wake up!" Glory kept her voice low, but with steel edges. "I've made a life for myself outside the compound. I came back to offer the same to you. Who's coming with me?"

"Where would we go?" Honor asked.

"What happened to you? Who cut your hair?" another woman whispered.

"Did you really kill the Nameless One?" someone else asked.

Questions surged around her, and Glory said, "Ssht. No time. If you're coming, we have to leave right now. If you don't come, you'll die. This building will blow up in twenty minutes."

"How do we know you're telling the truth?" a woman hissed.

"Yeah," the woman next to her chimed in. "They told us they captured you, and would make an example of you. You could be bait for a trap."

"A test to see if we fall for it," yet another woman broke in.

"Shut up, bitches. What do we bring?" Charity asked.

"Nothing. Everything will be taken care of," Glory replied.

"I'm in," Faith stuffed her feet into scuffed running shoes, tied the laces, and moved to Glory's side.

"Me too." Charity did the same.

"And me," Hope said.

"Anyone else?" Glory scanned the group, her heart aching, but understood speed was their only friend. If she took the time to try to convince the others, they'd all die.

The women looked away, and Glory turned to leave, flanked by Faith, Charity, and Hope.

"Me. I'm coming," Honor said and joined them. The other seven women melted back to their bunks. When Glory felt for their minds, their fear was thick and palpable. She pulled the dorm door open a shred and peeked. Alarms blasted her and she knew Roy and his men had launched their attack on the front door. Excellent timing. She and the women would have exactly what they needed: cover.

Honor cringed away from her. "This isn't safe."

"It's part of the plan," Glory said. "Men are helping me."

"What men?" Honor asked, her face a mask of indecision.

"No time. Come or stay." Glory sidled out the door with Faith, Charity, and Hope right behind her. By the time they reached the storage room and ducked inside it, Honor was with them once again. Glory wanted to hug her, but there wasn't time.

"Out the window." She pointed. "Once you hit the ground, run like hell for the tree line. Men will find you in about twelve minutes."

"What if they don't?" Hope's voice wavered a little.

"Then I will."

"You're not coming with us?" Faith asked, her forehead crinkled with worry.

"Nope. There's one thing I need to do." She motioned the women closer, barely breathing the words into their ears as she shared her plan. "Now get moving. We just wasted nearly a minute."

Without waiting to see her friends safely outside, Glory stole back into the hallway and ran for the stairs beyond the dorm. The door opened at her touch just as readily as the one next to the dormitory, and she made her way down spiral stairs leading a hundred feet underground. The Nameless Ones had buried the master computer deep to protect it. Fortunately, its location would protect her too, and give her the time she needed to absorb its information.

She hit the bottom of the stairs with five minutes to spare before Roy detonated the explosive to destroy the compound, at least its aboveground parts. She hoped he'd forgive her for being insubordinate, but if she missed this opportunity, there might never be another. Glory raced down a corridor, maximum power at the ready.

A double steel door blocked her way. She placed her palm over the scanner, but it didn't react; she hadn't expected it to. The Nameless Ones wouldn't have any of the women programmed into this particular palm reader. Stealth no longer mattered. She tuned her mind to the lock's frequency and tripped it, bolting through the door.

The single man stationed to guard the whirring bank of electronics surged to his feet, amber animal eyes flashing fury.

Glory beat him to the punch and battered him with a blast of electricity that would have flattened an elephant. He slumped to the floor.

She didn't waste time to make certain he was dead.

Tugging the fireproof door shut behind her, she opened her mind to the computer. It might shut down once it sensed the blast that was about to rip through the facility, and she wanted to get every scrap of data she could before that happened. Maybe if she was in control of it by then, she could force it to remain engaged until she was done.

It was tempting, so tempting to sort through the information flowing into her circuitry, but she ignored it, sucking down data in as big a dumps as the computer could spew. A muted blast battered her ears, followed by three more. The computer faltered and she pushed hard, willing it to continue to share its secrets.

"Yes!" She fist pumped the air as the information flow picked up again. Only a few more minutes, and she could take the escape tunnel the Nameless Ones had built from this room. She hoped to hell it hadn't been damaged by the blast, but it ran deep underground for a good hundred yards before exiting in the woods. She recalled when the men had built both it and this room, so proud of both accomplishments, they'd crowed to the skies.

And why not? No way would they think that information could ever be used against them. Certainly not by women they consistently underestimated.

She was grinning like a mad thing when she disconnected and blew through the lock on the room's only other door. Dust and dirt filtered through the tunnel's roof and an ungodly creaking noise lent wings to her feet. Glory raced up the tunnel. Once she cleared the area immediately beneath the compound, she'd be safe.

She hoped.

Sharp snapping right behind her was followed by an ominous boom, and the ceiling directly above where she'd been standing moments before crashed in, sending up clouds of grit and shaking the floor. Smoke filtered through the hole, tinged with flames, and she turned to stare at the destruction.

Not smart.

She spun, intent on flight, when the ceiling ahead of her shrieked in protest. She barely moved beyond its trajectory when it imploded too, showering her with fist sized stones.

The air was filling with smoke, and it was getting harder to breathe. She bolted up the gradually sloping passageway as if the hounds of Hell were snapping at her heels. What good would everything she'd gleaned from the computer do if she died before she could make sense of it and tell someone?

oy was pleased, extremely pleased. For once, an operation against the freaks had succeeded. The attack on the compound came off without a hitch, each demolition block of C4 detonating right on schedule. Over a hundred freaks lay dead in plain sight, and Roy didn't doubt there were at least that number buried in smoking rubble. So far, he hadn't identified any females, but he hadn't taken the time to look closely. That could happen once Glory was back by his side.

Roy tapped Charlie's shoulder, and the two men raced into the woods to the assigned pickup point. At first, he didn't see anyone, and then a tall, black-haired woman who looked a lot like Glory sidled from a thick stand of evergreens. "Are you Glory's friend?" she demanded, her voice shaking with fear. Light streamed from her, and Roy didn't doubt she'd cream him where he stood if he gave the wrong answer—or lied.

"Yes." Roy glanced at three other women, who joined the first. They could have been quadruplets with their matching rangy builds, dark hair, and green eyes. Dressed in thin T-shirts and pajama bottoms, they shivered in the chill night air. He waited through five long breaths, but Glory didn't materialize.

"Where is she?" he demanded.

One of the women walked closer. "I'm Faith. Glory had something else to do. She said she'd be here soon."

Roy didn't think; he reacted, grabbing Faith and shaking her. "Where is she?" he growled, ready to pound the truth from her if she didn't give it up any other way.

Charlie pulled him off. "Knock it off, boss. You're scaring her. Not a good idea. These gals can kill the same way Glory does."

"I'm Honor." The woman who'd spoken first stepped forward. "Glory said not to tell you until twelve forty."

"Charity," the third woman spoke up.

"I'm Hope," the last woman said. "Yeah, if it takes her longer than that, you'll have to dig her out."

"What the fuck?" Roy pounded a fist into the nearest tree.

Charlie said. "Breathe, bro. That's only ten more minutes."

Roy turned on him, seizing his friend by the upper arms. "Dig her out means underground. Ten minutes might mean the difference between suffocation and life."

"Good point," Charlie muttered and jerked away from Roy's iron grip. He faced the women. "You have to tell us now. Glory put her life on the line to save you. It's the least you can do."

The women exchanged glances, and Roy felt the zing of telepathic communication flowing between them. He should have tried to listen, but he was too spun out. Hope squared her shoulders. She was shivering. "Glory tapped into the main computer to find out about our origins. It's in a room a long way beneath the compound."

"No!" Roy shouted. "She'll never get out. We blew the place sky high."

"There's a tunnel," Honor said. "The men built it as an escape route in case they had to scrub the computer fast."

Charlie shoved a jacket and sweater he'd pulled from his field pack into the women's hands. "Where's the exit?"

"Somewhere in these woods." Honor shrugged into one coat and handed the other to Faith.

Fury mixed with despair filled Roy. To come so close, only to lose Glory was unacceptable, untenable, unthinkable. Why hadn't she told him about her plan?

Because I would have vetoed it. That's why. He groaned; it came out a wounded beast sound.

Milton Reins' voice filled his head all over again saying, "Lorna's gone, Roy. God, dear God, but I'm so sorry." He'd gone a little crazy after his wife had been executed, Mafia style, and almost the same thing was happening again. Dead was dead, whether from asphyxiation or a bullet. The edges of his vision grayed with misery.

He pushed his enhanced senses outward, seeking Glory's unique feel. Nothing. Maybe the tunnel was shielded with metal, which meant she was probably still in there. "Did we capture any of those bastards?" he asked Charlie.

"Yeah."

"Find a jacket for the other gals," Roy barked and took off at a hard run for his men. Barreling into them, he snapped, "Prisoners?"

"Over there." David pointed.

Roy glanced at the metal-barred enclosure containing two freaks. It had been risky not to kill all of them, but he'd thought if he kept at least a few alive, they might give up information about the location of the other compounds. He glanced from one dark haired man to the other. Much like the women, they could have been clones. Tall, thickly muscled, with dark hair and those weird animal eyes with the vertical slit pupils. Much like his men, they wore black from head to toe.

"I need information."

"Why would we tell you anything?" one of the men countered and drew his lips back in a snarl.

"For immunity."

The other man made a derisive snorting sound. "Like we'd believe you."

"Fine. Don't." Roy pushed into the man's mind, heedless of damage, and culled through his memories, ignoring his shrieks of pain.

"I'll tell you anything," he screamed, clearly in agony. "Just get out of my head." Blood poured from his nose and ears, and he held his skull in a death grip between his hands.

Roy withdrew, relieved his gambit had worked, but frantic about Glory. "Where does the tunnel from your main computer room exit?"

The man rattled off a series of coordinates. Roy translated them into a GPS location and bolted from the clearing as fast as he could go.

"Need a hand, boss?" David's voice rang after him.

"Sure," he called over one shoulder.

Roy located the hidden metal door easily and scraped debris from the forest floor and snow off it. He tugged, but it wouldn't open. When he bent close, he saw why. It was padlocked from this side, but Glory should have been able to defeat the lock—if she were still conscious. David hovered off to one side. "Want me to hit it with my Sig, boss?"

"I'll get it with mine," Roy said. By now, his anxiety about Glory had hit fever pitch. Since the door was locked, she had to be trapped on the other side. Everything he knew about poisonous gases from explosions displacing oxygen pulsed through his head. He pulled his gun, flipped off the safety, and blasted the lock.

It disintegrated, and David swarmed forward and pulled the door out of the way. Thick smoke billowed from the hole. "I'll get the O2," David said. "Looks like she's going to need it."

Silently blessing his man for loyalty and quick thinking, Roy flicked on his headlamp, took a deep breath, and dropped down a set of metal stairs. Once his feet hit the tunnel floor, he crab walked to take advantage of the clearer air near the floor, moving as fast as he could. The tunnel was narrow, not much more than eight feet across, so there'd be no way of missing her. Smoke and chemical gasses scoured his lungs. He coughed reflexively and pulled the lip of his turtleneck over his mouth and nose.

The tunnel turned a ninety degree bend and Roy moved forward. He couldn't see much more than a foot in front of him and nearly stumbled over an enormous chunk of what had to be the roof that had caved in. He crawled around it, only to find another, and another, crisscrossed by beams of timber that had probably supported the tunnel.

The clink of an oxygen tank hitting rock reached his ears before David caught up to him. The man turned. "Lash this across my back. Don't want to jostle it too much. I brought a pick and shovel with me too."

Roy wound straps from David's field pack around the O2 tank, and grabbed the shovel. "How'd you know to bring them?"

"I've worked mine accidents before. We need to hurry, boss. The air's bad down here, and it was a hell of a lot worse before we cracked the door."

With David helping, they cleared rubble. Each big piece they moved tore a strip from Roy's soul. He was afraid Glory would be beneath one of them. Finally, desperately afraid what he'd find, he felt for her energy. Relief sluiced through him when it pinged back at him, weak, but there.

Thank fucking Christ!

He should've hunted for her that way before, but using his augmented senses wasn't second nature. Knowing she was still alive would have saved him a shitload of angst, but if they couldn't locate her—and damned fast—she might not stay that way long. Something pale caught the glow from his headlamp, and he moved as quickly as he could around timbers canted at crazy angles and still settling rock piles.

"Help me," he called to David. "I see her hand sticking out. She's under this stack of crap."

"Careful," the other man cautioned. "We should radio someone to bring a backboard down here. She could have a spinal cord injury."

"Let's get all this off her first." Roy started with her upper body, carefully moving rocks and timber that had buried Glory. David worked his way up from her legs.

As soon as her head was clear, Roy placed a hand over Glory's neck. The faint beat of blood rushing through her carotid artery was the sweetest thing he'd ever felt. David unbuckled his pack and handed the oxygen over. Roy stabilized the plastic mask around her head and started gas flowing. Her color improved almost immediately, shading from white to pearlescent pink. Her respiration seemed better too.

The men went back to freeing her. Even with both of them working, it took close to half an hour to shift everything away from her body. Some of the pieces were so heavy, it required both of them working in tandem to budge them.

"About that backboard?" David hunkered next to Roy.

"Sure. Drive one of the cars close so we'll have it to load her in once we bring her out. That way we can at least get her out of the weather. Radio for a medevac unit while you're outside too. Your communications unit won't work in here."

"Ten-four." David scrambled down the passageway leaving Roy sitting in the dirt next to the woman he loved.

He stroked her hand, and then her grime-streaked face. "You're going to make it, goddammit. You understand?" he growled. "That's an order. You cannot fucking die on me."

She made a gagging noise. He ripped the mask off and turned her on her side. You weren't supposed to move suspected spinal cord injuries, but having her inhale her own vomit and choke to death wasn't smart, either. She puked bile into the dirt while he held her head.

"Sssh. It's okay. You're going to be fine. It's good to get that crap out."

She coughed, and coughed again, struggling weakly against his hold on her. "Let me sit," she croaked, her voice the barest rustle.

"I'm not sure that's a good idea. If your back was injured—"

"Not," she cut in. "Right leg's broken and maybe some ribs on my right side. I suppose they might just be bruised, but they hurt like a motherfucker. Nasty bump on my head. Maybe a concussion."

"Where'd you go to medical school?" he asked, his voice brusque to shield the riot of emotions pummeling him. She was awake, goddammit. Awake and talking and making sense. As close as she'd come to dying, it felt like divine intervention.

"We all learned emergency med tech stuff because none of us were MDs."

Roy could have hugged her, but he didn't want to injure her further. Hugs could wait until a bona fide medical professional cleared her. Instead, he bent and brushed his lips over hers. "You scared the shit out of me. If you weren't hurt, I'd turn you over my knee and spank you."

"Oooh, sounds kinky." Her lips twitched as if she were attempting a smile, but it turned into a grimace.

"Field agents do not make secret plans," he went on, tried to look stern, but failed utterly. He was so glad she was alive, he was sure it was stamped all over his face.

"I'm sorry, but I had to do this." She shoved hair out of her face, leaving grimy tracks from her fingers. "If I didn't do it now, I wouldn't have gotten another chance. The other compounds will mobilize…"

He laid a hand over her lips. "Hush. Save your strength. We'll have plenty of time to talk once you're out of here."

David and Charlie materialized with a backboard, and David reached to shut off the hissing O2 tank. "We heard you talking," Charlie said to Glory. "You being conscious so soon is excellent news. Now, let's get you out of here."

Between them, they got her strapped onto the board. Roy got the front, Charlie the back, and David stuffed the oxygen tank in his field pack. Roy had forgotten how many obstacles lay between them and the steps to the outside. Because they had to clear a path wide enough for the backboard again and again, it took them over an hour to move Glory into the still, cold air of very early morning.

The medevac chopper arrived and paramedics swarmed her, checking vitals, and hooking up an IV. "We're taking her to University Hospital in Seattle," the pilot told Roy.

"I'll get there as fast as I can," Roy said. "Post security. Call Langley for authorization if you need it, but I want a guard outside her room at all times."

"You got it, sir." The pilot, who looked about twenty, though he had to be older than that, snapped off a salute.

"Not bad." Charlie laughed. "You got military aspirations, young man?"

"You bet, sir." The pilot saluted again.

"Can we see her, please?" Honor moved toward Glory's backboard. "Just for a minute before you take her away?"

"Sure," Roy replied.

Faith, Hope, and Charity joined Honor, and they squatted next to Glory. Someone had found thick jackets for all the women. "Thank you, sister." Honor bent forward and kissed Glory's forehead.

"Yes, thank you so much," the others echoed.

"We'd be dead if it weren't for you," Faith said. "As soon as you're well, we'll all go out and celebrate."

"Sounds wonderful." Glory gazed from one woman's face to the next, tears shimmering in her eyes. "Thanks for believing in me. It would have been awful if none of you had come with me."

Each of the women followed Honor's lead and kissed Glory's forehead before straightening.

"I have to admit, I almost didn't." Honor laughed uncomfortably.

"I know," Glory said, and then called, "Roy?"

"Right here."

"Can you find space for my friends at Langley?"

He smiled. "Of course. They'll need a safe place to live."

"We get to stay together?" Faith asked, swallowing hard. "Getting out from under the Nameless Ones was gift enough, but that's icing on the cake."

"Oh my God, but that would be amazing," Charity said. She turned toward Roy and threw her arms around him. "Thank you, sir, whoever you are."

"You're very welcome." He stepped out of her embrace and shook a finger at her. "Don't think it will be a free ride. You've seen how hard I made Glory work."

"Looks to me like there's more to that story," Hope observed slyly. "And I want to hear every juicy detail."

"That'll cost you," Glory warned, her eyes dancing with merriment. "It will be great to have you guys close by."

"Yeah." Honor raised her arm and flexed a bicep. "We can form our own fighting unit."

Roy nodded knowingly. It appeared Glory wasn't the only augmented human not above helping herself to his thoughts. He furled his brows. "That's surprisingly close to the mark."

Honor grinned at him. "Really? How curious."

"Can we get rolling now, sir?" the pilot asked Roy. At his nod, the pilot and two paramedics loaded Glory into the chopper.

"If you want to fly back with her, boss—" David began, but Roy held up a hand to cut him off.

He'd like nothing better than to not let Glory out of his sight ever again, but he had unfinished work here. "Got to button this site up. Then we'll all head to Seattle and drive the hospital crazy until they release her."

He turned toward the chopper, ducked to avoid the wash from its slowly rotating blades, and clambered into the cockpit. "You take good care of her," he told the pilot. "She's part of my team."

"You got it, sir." Another sloppy salute made Roy smile. He

pushed past the pilot, deeper into the bird where he made his way to Glory's side. The paramedics shifted to make space for him.

"I'll get done here as soon as I can." He kneeled next to where her board was lashed to a platform.

"Do what you have to." She stroked the side of his face. "I would have made it out of that tunnel on my own, but the air just got worse and worse…"

"Sure thing, tiger." He ruffled her hair.

She wound a hand behind his neck and pulled him closer. "I love you. Thanks for rescuing me that night in the diner."

His throat thickened with emotion. "Just do everything the docs tell you. I need you on the mend and by my side."

"Aye-aye, sir."

He snorted laughter. "This ain't the Navy, sweetheart."

She started laughing too, but quit almost immediately and made a grab for her right side. "Ouch. That hurts."

"My fault. No more jokes." He leveled his gaze at her, hoping she could read how much she meant to him in the intensity flaring from his entire body.

"Maybe by the time you get to Seattle, I'll have had a chance to sort through what I downloaded from the computer." Her green eyes sheened with tears. "I need to know who I am, where I came from. I've felt like half a person these last seven years." One of the tears dripped down her cheek, tracking soot with it.

He kissed her forehead. "I understand better than you think. I've been less than half a person since Lorna died." He sucked in a breath. "Rest, Glory. Just rest. We'll have time for everything else."

"We almost didn't. You saved my life—again."

"Don't let it go to your head." He let his hand linger on her cheek for a moment. Then he got to his feet and made his way out of the helicopter. Roy watched as the rotors accelerated to traveling speed, and the bird soared skyward.

"Ready to sort through the rubble, sir?" David asked.

"Yes. Maybe we'll find more survivors, and where they kept the rest of their women."

Poking through carcasses was far from his favorite task, but Roy zipped into a full bodysuit, complete with visored hood, and followed his men into the wreckage of the freaks' compound. Depending on how gruesome it was, he'd water down what he told Glory.

CHAPTER 16

A weak December sun shone through the window of Glory's hospital room. Her ribs were only bruised, but her right fibula was indeed broken. Despite being hit in the head by falling debris, imaging studies didn't reveal any damage, and her headache had subsided after the first day or so. An orthopedic surgeon secured her broken bone with a pin, and she wore a removable walking cast on that leg made of foam, metal staves, and Velcro.

She'd spent five days in University Hospital and was healing quickly, one of the side benefits of her enhanced physiology. She'd caught enough snippets of conversations with her extra-sharp ears, when the doctors thought they were far enough away she'd never hear, to understand she needed to leave the hospital before they became even more intrigued by her physiology.

Now if I could just convince them of that... So far, they'd just nodded and made noncommittal comments whenever she asked about a release date.

Roy had visited her every day once he returned from the mountainside compound. The rest of the team boarded a military jet for Langley two days before, along with the women from her dorm. The only ones left on the west coast were her and Roy.

The time alone in the hospital had given her time to grieve for the seven women who'd refused to come with her. She hadn't let herself dwell on it that night because it would have gotten in the way of saving the women who trusted her enough to take a chance. And it would have compromised her ability to focus on draining the computer's brain.

She hadn't done much except sort the data she'd absorbed. Every single compound worldwide was stored in her brain, including the breeding farms destroyed during the rebellion. If she tracked her assigned number, she should be able to discover where she'd been created, and the humans whose DNA formed the substrate for her being. So far, she hadn't been ready to face that information, or much else about her origins, preferring to wait for when she had a more private environment. Now that she actually had the ability to do so, identifying her mother and father was frightening. After all, it was likely they were dead, particularly if they'd been part of the cohort of scientists targeted by the Nameless Ones.

Glory shook her head. *Nameless Ones*, her ass. They had both first and last names, but never shared them outside their own ranks. The other jewel from her time with the compound's computer was a comprehensive list of everything her augmented body was capable of. She'd only tapped far enough into it to discover the women's abilities far outstripped the men's because of the duplication of having two X chromosomes, where the men had one X and one Y.

A sharp tap on her door made her head snap up. Roy stood in the doorway, with a huge smile on his face. "Guess what, sweetheart? The docs say you're good to go." He strode to the bed and sat on its edge. "Personally, I think they want to get the guard out of their hallway, but let's not kick a gift horse in the shins."

"Mouth." She giggled. "It's not kick a gift horse in its mouth, whatever that means. Lots of your human sayings don't make a whole lot of sense to me."

"That one's pretty simple." He took her hand. "The original saying was don't look a gift horse in the mouth. One of the best ways of determining how old a horse is, and hence its relative value, was by looking in its mouth. That saying encouraged people to enjoy a gift, not be hung up on how much it's worth."

"Thanks for the parable lesson. Did they say exactly when I can leave?"

"Right now. They pulled your IVs this morning, so there's nothing holding you here. Get your street duds on, and we're out of here." He moved off the bed and shut the door to her room.

She cocked her head to one side. "I suppose you're going to stand there and watch me dress."

"Damn straight, sister."

"I am not your sister." Glory grinned.

"I'm most fully aware of that fact." Roy raked her from head to foot with his gaze; banked fires smoldered in the depths of his eyes. He opened the small closet and handed her a pair of dark slacks and a black wool sweater he'd brought for her a couple days before. The clothes she'd worn the night at the compound were so trashed, she'd asked the hospital staff to incinerate them.

She tossed back the covers and swung her legs over the side. After a pause, she limped to the small dresser that held her underwear and personal effects. Exquisitely aware of his eyes on her, she took a bit more time than necessary shrugging out of her backless hospital gown, hooking her bra, and working panties up her legs. Stretching the panties over the walking cast turned out to be a trick and a half. When he lent a hand, running his hand up her leg, desire jolted through her, adding a delicious sensitivity to her skin.

She eyed the waiting slacks and made her way to the room's only chair where she sat and undid the Velcro strips holding the cast in place. Once it was off, she pulled the pants up, balanced on her good leg to pull them over her butt, and sat back down to stuff her leg into the cast once again.

"How long will you need that thing?" he asked, and looked around. "I don't see any crutches."

"No crutches, and I'll only have the cast for three or four more days. I didn't really need the pin the docs repaired my leg with, but it seemed easier to go along with the program. Could you toss me my left boot from the closet? Maybe you could gather the rest of my stuff and put it in that duffel you have slung over your arm. I'd do it myself, but I'm anxious to get out of here."

Glory watched him go through the few cupboards and drawers in her room, chucking her pathetically few possessions into the duffel. She couldn't help herself, she started to laugh.

"What's so funny?"

"You're like a goddamned boy scout. Efficient as hell and ready for anything. By the way, where are we flying out of?"

"You'll see." A smile illuminated his face, making him even more striking. She couldn't stop looking at his shaggy black hair, strong-boned features, and dancing blue eyes.

She stood, albeit a bit unsteadily. "I'm ready. Don't I have to sign out or something?"

He shook his head. "Company agents have a few privileges. This is one of them. No hospital records."

"More like no records at all." She quirked a brow. "Do you guys even have fingerprints?"

"I'll never tell." Roy draped the duffel's strap over a shoulder and pulled the door open for her. "Turn right and go to the end of the hall where the elevator is."

When they got there and the elevator opened, Roy pushed the up button. She wanted to ask why the fuck they weren't going to wherever he had a car waiting, but kept her mouth shut. They got out on the top floor, and he shouldered open a door onto the roof. She limped after him and stopped when she came around a corner and saw a shiny black helicopter. It was much smaller than the one that had picked them up in Madison.

"Holy shit!" She pointed at the sleek craft. "That's what we're leaving in?"

He threw a mock hangdog look her way. "I'm crushed. We had a date. Did you forget?"

"Of course not, but I missed it. I was in the hospital the night you made us reservations at that bed and breakfast."

He took her hand and helped her inside the chopper. "I called them after you were hurt and left the date open. It's not prime tourist season, so they told me whenever we showed up would be fine, so long as they had a few hours' notice."

He got in the other side and took the left seat. She plucked a headset from the center instrument cluster and settled it over her head. "Can I fly?"

Roy burst out laughing. "Once I get us out of Seattle airspace, sure."

"Tell me about where we're going," she said as Roy fiddled with knobs, levers, and buttons, and the craft gained altitude.

"Let me radio our position and intended flight plan, then I will. Pay attention. If you want to learn to fly, those parts are almost as important as the physical aspects of making sure we don't crash."

She listened and watched as they flew west over Puget Sound and then north toward the San Juan Islands. He handed the controls over to her, and she delighted in the feel of the small helicopter beneath her fingertips, tapping into the onboard computer to become one with the chopper.

"You asked where we're going," he said. "It's a resort community called Rosario on Orcas Island. A retired agent and his wife run a very small operation there. They're absolutely trustworthy and specialize in providing a private retreat for agents who need a break."

"Sounds lovely." She tapped a GPS display with her index finger. "You already plotted our course."

"Yes." He winked. "It's that boy scout mentality."

"Aw, don't take that wrong. I love that part of you." She snorted. "I'm more like artificial intelligence than you could dream of being, despite those injections you had. If you weren't compulsive and organized, we'd never get along."

"Music to my ears." He placed a hand over the one she had balanced on the yoke and gazed at her through narrowed eyes. "You melded your brain with the onboard computer. It's why flying this thing is like yesterday's news for you."

"One of the things I found out from the compound's computer," she said, not exactly answering his question, "is that females have better innate abilities than males, but all that data was entered by the men. Given what happened when I worked with you and your team, my guess is the men didn't understand how to leverage their skills." She shrugged. "Maybe you need to trust your intuitive side to maximize the genetic manipulation's full potential."

A chortle burst past Roy's mouth. "First you play the boy scout card, and then the female intuition one." He rolled his eyes. "You never did answer me about merging with the on board computer."

She grinned. "Of course I did. Why wouldn't I? You could do the same thing. Go ahead," she urged. "Try it."

~

ROY DID, and he was still smiling.

Flying by the book, compared with flying as an extension of the aircraft's processing unit, were as different as night and day. He felt like an ass for not realizing even a hundredth of what the injections had done for him, but apparently the male freaks hadn't fully understood their capabilities, either. Settling the chopper gently inside the private Rosario resort, he cut the engine. When he pushed the door open, the salt tang of the sea bit into his nostrils, and he inhaled deeply. He came around, helped Glory out, and slung duffels around his shoulders.

"Give me the computer bag," she said. "I'm not a total invalid."

"This way." He steered her through a gate that led to a cottage overlooking the sound.

"Don't we have to check in or something?"

"Not here." He twisted the knob and pushed the cottage door

open, setting their things on the floor. Nothing had changed. Knotty pine lined both walls and ceiling. Paisley upholstered plush furniture was scattered around the room, interrupted by oak tables and antique oil lamps. A stone fireplace took up an entire wall.

She put his computer bag down and made her way to where he stood. "It's lovely. I wasn't trying to pry when I just peeked in your head—not exactly—but you've been here before."

He nodded. "It's a special place, but I've never brought anyone with me. Figured it was time to change that." Roy felt the touch of her mind in his, seeking, probing. She was subtle, but he knew the feel of her now.

"It's where you came after your wife died."

"I was here for months." He gazed at her. "It's where I found the will to go on."

"You've come back here when you needed to sort things out."

"Like I said, it's a magical place for me. Because it renews me, nourishes my soul, I thought it might be a perfect place for you to move past the deaths of your friends, and being a key element in our last operation."

"But I wanted to help." Her direct gaze faltered, and she studied the floor.

"Yes, and your help meant the only home you remembered—never mind how you felt about it—was obliterated from the face of the Earth."

Roy opened his arms, and she walked into them. "Thank you for understanding." Her voice was muffled against his shoulder. "You never told me what you found when you and the team went through what was left."

"And I'm not going to now, either. It can wait until we're back at Langley."

She tilted her head so she could look at him. "Usually I'd fight you on a decision like that, but not this time."

"It cuts both ways," he said. "You understand what I struggle with too. Can you walk well enough to take a stroll down the beach?"

"Sure. If you don't mind going slow."

He let go of her and tipped her chin up with a finger. "I'll have you jogging ten miles again in no time."

"Thanks, coach."

He took her hand, and they walked out double sliding glass doors and onto a private stretch of beach that extended a quarter mile. Clouds that would create a glorious sunset filled the sky. A brisk breeze tugged the surf into whitecaps, and a pungent salt smell coated everything.

"I thought we'd fall into the first bed we found," she said as she walked by his side, leaning into him, "but this is good too."

"Never fear about the bed part. We'll get there. I wanted to make certain you had space to talk with me about what happened if you needed to."

"I've thought about it a lot, and I'm not sure what to say."

"I've lived with death for a lot of years." Roy considered his next words carefully. "I've never gotten used to it. I always second guess what I could have done differently. Mostly, I wanted you to know I'll never judge you, and I'm always here to listen."

"I thought about you while I was in the hospital. About us, actually." Her voice faltered before she went on. "I love you for caring about me, Roy." She stopped walking, and he turned to face her just before he closed his mouth over hers. She kissed him back and twined her arms around him, clinging to him as if her very existence depended on it. He recognized that desperation because it was the same way he felt about her.

Time stopped as they held one another, kissing like they were the last two people left on Earth. Sexual need braided with something much deeper: love and caring, and Roy knew he'd spend the rest of his life with the woman folded into his arms—if she'd have him.

Breathless, they separated, gazing into one another's eyes. "Make love with me." She moved her hand between them and curved it around his erect cock.

"No condoms. They're back in the cottage."

"We can improvise."

"There's a gazebo just around this stretch of shore. It has blankets and will get us out of the wind." He wove his arm around her waist.

"Sounds wonderful."

It was farther than he remembered, and he worried about her leg, but she kept a slow, steady pace. When they got there, he lit the brazier and made them a nest in front of floor to ceiling glass windows with blankets that smelled of the sea. Laying her in the center of the blankets, he tugged off the one shoe she wore and removed the walking cast.

She unzipped her jacket, folded it beneath her head for a pillow, and pulled her top off over her head. Roy barely recognized the inchoate moan that filled the small space as his, but he surged forward and filled his hands with her breasts, rubbing, teasing her nipples into stiff peaks.

She reached for his thick, woolen jacket, but couldn't get it off his shoulders. Reluctantly, he let go of her, and stripped off his clothes, starting with kicking off ancient running shoes. She undid her pants and pushed them down her hips along with her panties.

"I wanted to do that," he said, stepping out of his worn jeans.

"We can undress each other once I'm more mobile." Glory opened her arms, and he lay next to her and stroked stray hairs back from her face. Next, he traced the line of her cheekbone out to her ear. "You're so perfect."

"I was designed that way." She smiled, the depths of her soul shining from her eyes. "You got it naturally."

Something almost painful shifted inside him, the door he'd buried his humanity behind, but he kicked it wider, wanting to let her into his secret places—all of them. She shifted onto her side and kissed him, licking his lips to encourage him to open his mouth. Roy gathered her into his arms, stroking his fingertips down the silk of her skin.

She ran her nails down his back, grazing him lightly, before snaking a hand between their bodies to curl her fingers around his erection. He cupped her ass and moved his hand between her legs, finding her already slick with wanting him. Because reaching around her was awkward, he turned them until she was on her back, moved his mouth from hers and captured a nipple. A delighted little trill rolled from her throat, and she tightened her hold on his shaft.

Roy rubbed her slick nubbin as she arched into his touch. He rubbed harder, faster, and she dissolved in an orgasm, her hips bucking beneath his fingers. When a second peak followed on the heels of her first, it was all he could do to hold himself back. Her fingers had quickened their tempo to match his. He placed a hand over hers. "I don't want to come quite yet, sweetheart."

Her beautiful green eyes flickered open and searched his face. Lips curving in the softest of smiles, she scooted out of his embrace and downward, licking as she went. When her tongue grazed the tight buds of his nipples, his balls tightened. Feeling the heat of her breath move across his belly set every single nerve ending on fire.

Glory closed her mouth over his glans, experimentally. She tilted her head away from him long enough to say, "You'll have to help me. I've never done this before."

"You'll figure it out. Jesus, but you feel amazing."

"Keep the praise coming, Kincaid." She shot him a wanton grin before settling in to work him with her mouth and hands. He felt her slip inside his mind again, joining with him, and understood how he felt in her mouth, how he tasted, and how hot sucking him off made her. He wanted to turn her so he could tease her clit with his tongue at the same time.

"Afterward," she spoke into his mind. *"This is just for you."*

He tried to formulate an answer, but he was too far gone. Since she had a built-in feedback loop, she was able to heighten his arousal until he was on the verge of coming, and then back things off, skimming along the edge of ecstasy. When he finally came, she held him close drinking down everything that pumped from his aching balls.

She let go of him and rested her head on his chest with his fingers still tangled in her hair. "I don't have words for how high you took me," he murmured once he could talk.

"You don't need any."

"Guess not, since you were inside my head." He moved a hand to her breast. "Would you like more loving?"

"Of course, but maybe back in the cottage." She made her way to the head of their impromptu bed, dragging more of their discarded clothes to pile beneath their heads. "Oh my!" She pointed out the glass doors in front of them and wriggled to a sitting position.

He'd had eyes only for her. When he followed the direction of her finger, he saw the winter sky shot with blue, hot pink, and deep purple. "Beautiful. Just like you."

"Too bad they never last very long." She gazed wistfully at the shifting shades of the sunset.

"We can cheat." He sat cross-legged next to her and grinned.

"What do you mean?"

"Let's get back in the bird. We'll chase the sunset. By the time we come back, the innkeepers will have left supper in our cottage."

Her eyes lit with anticipation, and she started pulling clothes on. "Do you make a habit of chasing sunsets?"

Roy nodded. "Sure. Rainbows too. And unicorns. Once, I was so taken with the colors I didn't watch my fuel gauge and nearly didn't make it back to land." He sorted clothing, slipping things back on.

Glory got to her feet. "I wish I could race you, but that'll have to wait."

Roy hugged her, and held the door open. "Everything can, so long as we're together."

She stopped outside the gazebo, her face solemn. "There are things we have to talk about."

"They can wait too. Until we're back at Langley."

CHAPTER 17

Glory glanced around her small apartment at Langley. She and Roy had arrived late last night after three idyllic days in the San Juans. He spent last night with her, before leaving for his own quarters to clean up and get fresh clothes. She walked with a slight limp as she finished getting ready for a seven a.m. meeting, but no longer needed the walking cast.

It had been easy to maintain the *no yesterdays* and *no tomorrows* agreement while they were at the cottage, but they couldn't hold the world at bay forever. She'd known it then, and it was doubly clear now.

She clumped to the door and headed for the elevator, ready to get this next part over with. Faith, Hope, Honor, and Charity would join them, but not for the first hour. Their apartments were in the next building. She'd wanted to visit with them last night, but it was past midnight, and she hadn't wanted to disturb their rest.

Glory made her way to a meeting room in the same building where Milton's office was. When she arrived, Roy and Milton were already there, and the remainder of the team was dribbling in. She poured herself a cup of coffee and set it in front of a seat at the table.

"You're not getting off that easy, young lady," Uncle Miltie said. "Today, you're up here right next to me." He jerked his chin at an empty chair.

"Yes, sir." She moved her coffee.

"Glad to see you're mostly recovered," he went on, and cast a significant glance Roy's way. "Nothing like a little beach therapy."

The corners of her mouth twitched into a smile. "Guess that means you've been there too."

"We all have," Charlie cut in. "This job's hard."

Everyone was seated before seven. Milton cleared his throat. "You all know that Glory raided the computer at the Pacific Northwest compound. Time for us to hear what she found."

Glory pressed her lips together to keep them from trembling. This was it. Once she was done, it would truly be the death knell for those like her who refused clemency—if it was even offered.

She straightened her shoulders. "I know where all the compounds are. Before I download the locations onto a map, I want to know if any of the…" she faltered, not quite sure what to call the genetically altered humans anymore. "…residents will be given a choice."

"Are you asking if we'll extend an offer for them to work for us rather than against us?" Milton asked.

"Yes. Of course, some will grab it and not be telling the truth. Their hatred runs deep."

"It does complicate things," Milton said, watching carefully for her reaction. "Plus, they can kill my people with their thoughts unless we swathe them in steel cages."

"I understand if the answer's no." Glory clasped her hands behind her.

"You're jumping to conclusions." Milton kept his gaze on her. "It may surprise you, but I've discussed this with my superiors, because the same concern occurred to me. We agreed to blanket the media with bulletins. Any freak who surrenders voluntarily by January fifteenth will be offered asylum until we figure out how to best use his or her talents—and if we can trust them."

Glory narrowed her eyes. "That's very generous of you, and it'll work fine for the men. The women will see it since they have free access to the Internet, but they aren't allowed freedom to come and go without an escort."

"The thing about plans is they always require backup plans." Milton nodded, and she could almost feel his mind churning, but resisted the temptation to peek. "Let's see what sort of numbers— and the gender split—we net this way," he said after a short pause.

"Not that you need my agreement," Glory glanced at Milton, "but the best plans always require more data. I'd like to float an idea before I download those compound locations." Her voice was louder than she meant it to be, and she dialed it back a notch. "Requesting permission to form a unit with the four women from my compound. We can do the same thing I did. Hit the compounds before you do and see which women want to come with us."

"How will you find them?" Charlie asked. "This time, you knew the layout."

"The compounds are all built from the same schematics," she replied, and smothered a wry grin. "Remember, we were patterned after computers, so we found something functional and repeated it." She sucked in a breath. "If this works, we'll develop quite the commando squad of women. Once it's over, they can all work for you." She smiled brightly at Uncle Miltie.

He burst out laughing. "Christ on a crutch, Glory. If they're all as headstrong as you, they'd drive me into an early grave."

"Understood, sir." She tried but couldn't quite stop smiling.

"Your plan's incomplete." Roy spoke as if it cost him.

"Why's that?"

"You never saw a large portion of the compound. When we walked the wreckage, we identified four pods where women lived." Roy looked away, and she girded herself, knowing whatever came next would tug at her heartstrings.

"Go on." She stood motionless, waiting.

"One of the pods included children, judging from what we found. Another had a stainless steel chiller that was still intact. Inside it, we found an array of fertility drugs used for artificial insemination."

Glory swallowed hard, and then did it again. "You're saying they ran a breeding farm in another part of the compound."

"It's exactly what he's saying," Charlie cut in. "He didn't want to tell you, but the rest of us convinced him he had to."

Glory dove into data she'd downloaded from the compound's computer. It didn't take long to corroborate the men's impressions. She pushed her emotions deep and stood straight. "Good news, actually. It means we can hit all four pods at every compound. Maybe we'll get lucky and find some children that are young enough not to carry permanent scars from these last seven years."

Roy locked gazes with her from across the table, and she sensed pride flowing from him. It touched her, and made her realize she wanted him to be proud of her, to see her as an asset, not someone he had to coddle and protect.

Something a little different—admiration—shone from Milton's dark eyes. He switched on a nearby computer with a touch screen, and a map of the world flickered to life on the display at the far end of the room. Milton swiveled the laptop to face her. "Show us where the compounds are."

She touched place after place, making small adjustments if she missed the mark by a slight margin. When she was done the map was lit with nearly fifty shining points of light. Rapid intakes of breath whooshed around the room. Clearly no one had expected nearly this many.

"A few," she touched half a dozen places, "were destroyed during the rebellion." She inhaled deeply, blew it out, and did it again. "This is where I came from." She tapped the light over Missoula, Montana.

Roy caught her eye again and said, "Ask him."

Milton turned to stare at her. "Ask me what?"

It was hard to breathe around the ball of anxiety lodged in her throat. "Since the government created me, they'd have kept at least some records—I hope. It didn't make sense to dredge through an entire database, but I've narrowed it down to a single site. I want to see my records. Know who the sperm and egg donors were."

"That wasn't in the information you got from the compound's computer?"

"I thought it was, but when I looked deeper I discovered their recordkeeping began after the rebellion. The location for all the breeding farms destroyed during the rebellion was there, but that's where the data stream stopped. My records at the compound only identified the farm I came from, nothing further."

"I'll do what I can to get you access," Milton said. The corners of his eyes crinkled with compassion. "Don't expect too much. As I recall, most of the genetic material came from the scientists and they're dead, and all the records of the exact sequence of genetic manipulations were destroyed."

"Maybe it's silly, but I've been fixated on discovering who I am ever since I realized I couldn't remember anything from before the rebellion."

"What else did you glean from the compound's computer?" Milton asked, apparently done talking about her.

"I got a lot more information about the limits of what I can do. And the differences between the men and women. Probably the best thing is for me to merge with one of your mainframes and do a data dump. I'm not sure how much of the information is readily transferrable to the men who've had the injections, but probably much more than you're using now."

"Done," Milton said. "Do any of you have questions?"

"Yeah," Charlie spoke up. "I have one. Boss isn't going to like it much." His gaze skittered to Roy. "I love having Glory on our team, but she and Roy are...close. How's that going to work?"

"She'll form her own team, heading up the women," Roy said. "That way she won't be in a direct line reporting to me." Glory swung her head to stare at him, but he held up a hand. "We haven't talked about this, but I knew it was a problem, so I came up with a solution."

"It's the CIA way," Milton chuckled softly, "except you also didn't run it past me."

"Oops, my bad." Roy shot a sunny smile at his boss.

"It's a good thing you're competent, Kincaid," Milton growled.

"Cute too," Roy murmured.

Milton rolled his eyes. "Back on track here. I'll get those notices cooking immediately. They should start hitting every major media source within the hour. What I want to avoid is all those compounds," he waved a hand over the lit-up map, "mobilizing against us simultaneously."

David whistled. "Hell, it could be WWIII, except we'd be fighting a race of super humans."

"Exactly," Milton said. "I like Glory's idea of shaping the women into their own unit. Any idea how long that might take?" he asked her.

"Hey, it was my idea too," Roy protested.

"Yeah, but she beat you to the punch floating it," Milton said, and focused on Glory. "Answer my question."

"Not long. We practiced together almost every day in the arena at the compound."

"Are you any good with weapons?" Charlie asked.

Glory grinned. "Sure, the built-in ones. Not so great with firearms, but it's simply a matter of plotting a bullet's trajectory. We can learn." She glanced at the wall clock, which read zero seven fifty. "The other women will be here very soon. Why don't we ask them?"

As if her words were prophetic, a sharp rap rattled the door. Milton got to his feet and opened it to let them in. They had scanner access to parts of the campus, but meeting rooms like this one were currently off limits.

The four women walked in. Honor wore a long black skirt and teal tunic; the others had chosen dark slacks and gray sweaters.

Glory nodded to herself. It was similar to how they'd dressed in the compound—all except for Honor.

Charity hesitated for a moment and then beat a path to Glory's side and swept her into a hug. "It's good to see you, hon."

"You too." Glory embraced her friend.

"Stop hogging her," Faith said.

"Yeah, I want a hug too," Hope cut in.

"And me," Honor echoed.

ROY WATCHED the exchange between the women, deeply glad at least a few of Glory's bunkmates had followed her out of the compound. Tears streaked the women's cheeks as they murmured to one another.

"We can do this later." Glory's voice rose above theirs. "Grab coffee and sit. We have things to decide."

She swiped at her damp face and waited until everyone had found a place at the table before outlining her offer. "...Of course you don't have to do a thing," Glory finished. "I'd love to have you work with me as free women, not because you feel coerced in any way."

"It's exciting," Honor said.

"Yes," Faith seconded. "Maybe we could rescue fifty of us, or a hundred."

"Wouldn't that be incredible?" Charity blinked away tears that sheened her green eyes.

"Even if we only rescued one, it would be worth it," Hope said, sounding fierce.

"What do we have to do?" Charity zeroed in on Roy, probably because she remembered him from that night at the compound.

"Don't look at me." Roy pointed at Milton. "He runs things around here."

"Okay." Charity turned to face him. "Same question."

"Technically, all you women need a college degree, but I can get that waived. Do you speak any other languages?"

"All of them," Glory said.

"Yes, we read grammar and syntax from the mind of whomever we're talking with," Honor added.

Milton drew his brows together and looked at the men. "You've had the injections. Can you do that?"

"No idea." Roy shrugged. "But I'm anxious to get my hands on that list of skills, talents, and abilities once Glory makes it available.

Conversation ebbed and flowed until Milton informed them lunch would be served in the underground practice area. Glory smiled at the women. "Guess that means we're going to get down and dirty this afternoon."

"Crap!" Honor glanced at herself. "I never get to wear skirts."

"I'll go with you to change," Glory offered. "That way I can show you where the practice area is."

"We'll all go," Hope said, "but we don't need your directions. I've absorbed a map of this place."

Roy watched them leave the room, and turned to face Milton. "It's a whole new ball game out there."

"No shit." Uncle Miltie snorted. "Shouldn't take much talking to get the brass to agree to sign them on as full agents, rather than special civilian ones. Never would have believed it, but we can learn a lot from them."

"I'm looking forward to it," Charlie cut in. "Never thought I got enough bang for my buck out of those damned injections."

"Yeah, and they hurt like a motherfucker," David muttered to the accompaniment of a chorus of assent from the other men at the table.

"Shall we hit the practice area, gentlemen?" Milton rose.

"Mind if I have a quick word?" Roy asked.

Milton furled his brows. "If you must. You are such a pain in the ass, Kincaid. We'll catch up with the rest of you shortly."

Roy waited until the men filed out, and the door closed behind them. "You dunned me for not telling you about my plan for Glory to head up her own team," he told Milton.

"Out with it." Milton crooked two fingers his way. "What else haven't you told me?"

"I'm going to ask her to move in with me. Assuming things work, I'll ask her to become my wife."

"Does she know?"

"Probably, since she's inside my head—a lot."

"But you haven't talked about it."

"Not yet. She needed to get through today before I piled more on her plate." Roy paused a beat. "And I wanted to keep our time in the San Juans as clear from anything but living in the moment as I could."

Milton cocked his head to one side. "The mind-meld stuff must add a whole new dimension."

"It does." Roy met his boss's gaze. "You do realize she just offered up her people to us. That can't have been easy, no matter how she feels about them."

"I get it, Kincaid. And I'll do everything in my power to see she has access to her roots." He shook his head. "I hope there's something there for her to look at. As I recall, there wasn't much left once the freaks got through annihilating the breeding farms."

"Thanks." Roy turned to leave.

"One more thing." Milton's voice stopped him, and Roy faced his boss. "I'm glad someone touched your heart again. I've been worried about you ever since Lorna was killed."

Roy felt sheepish as he admitted, "Yeah, I've worried about me too."

"Enough of this chick flick." Milton made a disgusted snorting noise. "Get moving, Kincaid. I'll stand you to a match on the mat after lunch."

"If it's too soon after lunch, I may puke on you."

"I'll take my chances."

CHAPTER 18

Glory sat in a small room poring over old compressed computer files that had been relegated to an electronic slag heap. It took Milton a week to secure permission for her to do this, and she didn't want to waste any of the hour she'd been given to search for her origins. Her fingers flashed over the keyboard as she sorted through reams of data.

Finally, what she needed flared to life on the screen, and she absorbed the names and backgrounds of her parents. They'd indeed been scientists—well-known ones, not residents at the compound. Excitement spread, warming her, as she continued to pull data. Both her parents had received Nobel prizes, her mother in chemistry, and her father in genetic research. No wonder they'd been willing to donate their DNA to what they must have viewed as a worthy cause.

A muted tap sounded on the door just before Roy pushed it open. "I can come back if you're still hunting."

"It's all right. I found what I was looking for. My father died last year from a hemorrhagic fever he caught in Africa, but Mother's still alive." An uncomfortable feeling twisted Glory's stomach into a knot. "What if I show up on her doorstep, and she tells me to go away?"

"Maybe you might want to start with a phone call or an e-mail."

"Yeah, you're probably right." She slumped against the chair's back. "I don't have to figure everything out right now. Maybe she never even knew she had children. It was my dad who was the geneticist."

"I can scarcely see him sneaking eggs from her ovaries without her knowing about it."

"There is that." Glory stifled a grin. Roy had a pointed way of cutting to the heart of things that was both funny and cynical at the same time. "Although, she might not know any of those eggs turned into living beings." Glory pressed her lips together. "I'm stalling, but there's really no rush on tracking her down. She's only fifty-eight. Not in danger of dropping dead tomorrow."

Glory closed her files down. Each of the other women had demanded a turn, so the computer archives would be busy for the rest of the day. "Let me alert Faith that she's up next, and then I'll leave with you."

She poked Faith telepathically, got to her feet, and made her way around banks of machinery to where Roy stood framed in the doorway. When she pushed toward his mind, she couldn't get in and felt taken aback he'd shielded it. All the men had improved their mental powers by leaps and bound in the last week, but he'd never barred her from his head.

"I have news," he said, "but I want to tell you about it, not have you dig it out of my mind."

She hooked a hand beneath his arm, and they walked down a cluttered corridor to a door leading out into a cold, sunny winter day. "Tell me what you didn't want me to discover on my own," she demanded, once they were outside.

"The docs think they can open that gated place in your brain. They found an area in their imaging studies that doesn't look like everything else—or like anything they've ever seen before. The other women have it too. Anyway, the neurosurgeons suggested dissolving it with a laser."

She crinkled her brow, thinking. "Does it have risks?"

"Of course. Anytime they muck around in your body there are risks."

"Mmph. The main reason I wanted it gone was to resurrect the missing pieces of my life, but knowing where I was created and who my parents are is probably enough. I'd still like to take a trip to Montana and look at whatever's left of the research center, but that doesn't have to happen anytime soon."

Relief washed over his features, and he exhaled sharply. "I was hoping you'd say that. I've known about the docs' opinion since yesterday, but I didn't want to say anything until I sorted out how I felt." He draped an arm around her shoulders.

"I'll think about it, but right now my answer would be no."

"Thank God. I like you how you are just fine, but this has to be your choice. I'm not the one with amnesia."

"Now you just like me?" she teased. "Here I thought it was more than that." She glanced at their trajectory. "Where are we going?"

"To a private place where we can sit and talk."

"Isn't the whole of Langley bugged?"

Roy laughed. "Not all of it." He tugged open the passenger side of a nearby car. "Would madam care for a ride?"

She got in, laughing along with him. Just being with Roy made her heart glad. Even though she didn't report to him anymore, but to Milton, he still oversaw much of the training and group exercises for her and the women. Roy had a sharp eye. He pushed them even further than they thought they could go. But then, he'd studied the information about abilities, talents, and skills she'd stolen so thoroughly, she was certain he had it memorized.

He pulled the car up in the older part of downtown McLean, Virginia. After helping her out, he left it with a valet. "Thought you might appreciate a late lunch," he said and steered her inside a small restaurant. It was tastefully decorated with white tablecloths and shiny crystal and silver on the tables.

"Right on time, sir." A smiling maître d' led them to a table tucked away in the back and held her chair for her. Bald and middle-aged with a kindly, lined face and cheerful brown eyes, he wore a dark jacket, white shirt, and dark pants.

"How'd you know who we were?" Glory blurted.

"Because Mr. Kincaid stopped in yesterday and made all the arrangements for this luncheon. I'll return presently with menus and a little wine to get you started."

"I feel underdressed," Glory told Roy. "If I'd had a little advance warning, I could have—"

"I don't care what you wear." His voice was thick with emotion, which surprised her. "It's you I want with me, not a chi-chi dress."

To cover sudden awkwardness that hovered between them, she murmured, "Good to know," unfolded her napkin across her lap, and waited. It was tempting to peek inside his head, but maybe he still had his wards up.

The maître d' returned with menus, a bottle of red wine, and two long-stemmed glasses. "The nineteen sixty-eight cabernet, just as you requested, sir." He poured a small swirl of wine, and once Roy had tasted it and nodded, the man filled both glasses partway and left.

Roy held up his glass. "To us."

"Isn't the return expression, I'll drink to that?" She clinked her glass against his before taking a sip. Not that she was any judge, but the wine was excellent, smooth and rich with hints of oak and blackberries.

"Indeed, it is." He drank, then set his glass on the table and fumbled in a jacket pocket.

"What's this?" She turned the small, black box he'd pushed her way over in her hands. "Some new sophisticated weaponry? A communicator? Except we scarcely need external ones anymore."

"Open it." He sounded as if he were strangling.

She pried the box open and gasped at the large shiny stone, surrounded by a phalanx of smaller ones, set in the most beautiful ring she'd ever imagined. Not understanding, she looked at Roy. "It's stunning, but—"

"I'm not making a very good job of this." He cleared his throat and took another sip of wine. "I want you to be my wife. It's an engagement ring, a promise between us."

"But you don't know me very well. Hell, I'm just figuring out who I am. How can you be sure?"

"I've asked myself that." He reached for her hand and squeezed it hard. "What I came up with is this is one of those things that will never have a rational answer. I love you, Glory. Please say yes. We don't have to get married tomorrow, but until we do, I'd—"

A tear formed in the corner of one of her eyes, followed by another on the other side.

"Aw, crap." He looked away. "I've made you cry. I'm sorry. Guess this was premature, but I'd hoped—"

She leaned close and kissed him, cutting off his words. "Women cry when they're happy too. I'm thrilled, blown away." She threw her arms around him. Her chair unbalanced and would've fallen if he hadn't caught it. "Of course I'll marry you."

"Really?" The harsh planes in his face fell away, leaving naked, unbridled joy.

"Really."

Roy let out a whoop that brought the maître d' to their table double time. "Sir?"

"Everything's fine. The lady just agreed to become my wife."

The maître d' broke into a grin. "That just might call for champagne on the house. I'll bring you a bottle straight away." He trotted toward the kitchen.

"Aren't you going to try it on?" Roy asked.

For a moment, she was confused; then she realized he meant the ring. She tugged it gently off its velvet pillow and turned it this way and that, enjoying the way light bounced from its facets. "Which finger? Surely it'll fit one of them."

"Third one on your left hand."

She slipped the ring on. It caught for a moment on her knuckle before sliding into place. "Perfect." She held her hand up, admiring the way the ring looked. "I've never had any jewelry, only seen it on television and the Internet."

He clasped her hand in his. "If you don't like it, or want to shop for something together, we can do that."

Glory shook her head. "It's wonderful. I love it because you chose it for me."

"You probably won't want to wear it in the field. It could catch on things, compromise you, but your wedding band will be flat so it won't get in the way."

A flutter in her belly warmed her, and she gazed into his sea-blue eyes. "There you go, planning ahead again."

He ducked his head, and color stained his tanned cheeks. "Sorry. I've spent so many years weighing every alternative that it's a tough habit to break."

"It's the second time you've apologized to me. Stop it. I was teasing you, not complaining."

The waiter delivered an ice bucket with a champagne bottle perched in its center and popped the cork. He did his best, but some of the bubbly ended up on the carpet. He poured two flutes for them and said, "Let me be the first to congratulate you on your upcoming nuptials. Have you picked a date?"

"The sooner the better," Glory said, delighted by Roy's broad smile. She lowered her voice to a conspiratorial tone and leaned toward the waiter. "He has to sneak into and out of my room at night. Once we're married, we won't have to do that anymore."

"I see." The waiter hid a chortle behind his raised hand and beat a hasty retreat.

"What'd I say?" Glory asked Roy.

"You made it sound like you're still living with Mom and Dad, and I crawl through your window every night."

She cocked her head to one side. "If you substitute The Company for Mom and Dad, I wasn't so far off the mark."

"I do not crawl through your window."

"No, but you wait until late enough you hope no one will notice. I'll bet that guard in the lobby knows plenty."

Roy handed one of the flutes to her. "Let's drink to our future, then there's something else I want to talk about."

She clinked her glass against his and drank, enjoying the flick of tiny bubbles against the sides of her mouth, tongue, and throat. Glory set her flute down and eyed the two liquor bottles on their table. "We'll get drunk if we finish both of these."

"No one says we have to finish them. Have as much as you want. Whatever we leave will be welcomed by the kitchen staff."

"They drink the guests' leftovers?" When he nodded, she asked, "How do you know that?"

"Because I worked my way through college—and law school— waiting tables."

Glory reached for his hand and threaded her fingers with his. "There's a whole lot I don't know about you."

"We have years for me to fill in the details. Or you could simply help yourself."

"I like it better when you tell me things. I feel less like a snoop. What else was on your agenda?"

Roy snorted. "This isn't a business meeting, sweetheart."

"Look, this whole human thing will take time. Okay?"

"Okay." He squeezed her hand. "Now that you've agreed to marry me, would you consider moving into my house?"

"But The Company gave you a smaller place than they gave me. It makes more sense for you to move in with me."

Roy switched back to the claret-colored wine and drank deep. Setting the glass down, he said, "I should have been clearer. I have a house here in McLean, Virginia. It's a few miles from The Company's campus."

Glory digested the information. "You have two houses?"

"Actually, I have three. There's another in the Florida Keys that I visit in the winter when I'm sick of the cold. You said you wanted to get married soon. If we do, we could go there for our honeymoon. It's quite pleasant this time of year."

She sipped her wine. Unused to alcohol, she felt a buzzing across her forehead, and her thoughts weren't quite as nimble. She set her glass down. "I'm not sure how to frame this, but I'm pretty sure the ring you just gave me is a diamond. They're expensive. Now you tell me you have two houses plus the one at Langley…"

"I'm far from wealthy," he cut in after her voice trailed off.

"Thanks for saving me from figuring out how to ask." She shook her head. "I'm never sure if what comes out of my mouth will offend someone."

"I'm the last person you need to worry about offending." He stroked the back of her hand. "I'm not rich by American standards, but I am comfortable. Haven't had much to spend my money on, so I've been saving for years."

"That's not important to me. I'd love you even if you were poor, just like me."

Roy got to his feet, pulled her out of her chair and swept her into a hug. When she angled her face, he kissed her long and deep.

The maître d', who'd been headed their way, spun on his heel.

Glory broke their kiss. "The waiter, he probably wants to take our order."

"Are you hungry?" Roy caressed the side of her face, his eyes brimming with love.

"Not particularly."

"Then he can wait."

Roy closed his mouth over hers again, and Glory kissed him back.

She was a lucky woman, no two ways about it. Her past had been harsh, but because of it, she'd treasure every single moment of her future.

~

You've reached the end of *Winning Glory*. This story continues in *Honor Bound*. Read on for a sample.

ABOUT THE AUTHOR

Ann Gimpel is a USA Today bestselling author. A lifelong aficionado of the unusual, she began writing speculative fiction a few years ago. Since then her short fiction has appeared in a number of webzines, magazines, and anthologies. Her longer books run the gamut from urban fantasy to paranormal romance to science fiction. Once upon a time, she nurtured clients. Now she nurtures dark, gritty fantasy stories that push hard against reality. When she's not writing, she's in the backcountry getting down and dirty with her camera. She's published over 50 books to date, with several more planned for 2018 and beyond. A husband, grown children, grandchildren, and wolf hybrids round out her family.

Keep up with her at www.anngimpel.com or http://anngimpel.blogspot.com

If you enjoyed what you read, get in line for special offers and pre-release special reads. Sign up for Ann's newsletter on her website or her blog.

HONOR BOUND

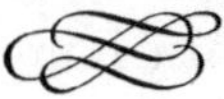

GEN TECH REBELLION, BOOK TWO

ilton Edward Reins III ducked and wove, staying one step ahead of the game—barely—while Honor and Charity, two genetically enhanced women, came at him from different directions. They were sparring in the workout arena located beneath the CIA compound in Langley, Virginia, a room as familiar as his office since he spent so much time there. He leaped, spun, and landed harder than he would've liked on the mat. At least he was still on his feet. Air whistled between his teeth. He grunted with effort and raised his arm to fend off Charity's forward drive.

He used her momentum to unbalance her enough she stumbled. Once she was out of the action at least for a moment, he pivoted in time to meet Honor head on. She threw all her weight forward. When that didn't work, she jumped on him, and wound her long legs around his waist while she pummeled his shoulders and back with karate chops. The points of her breasts pushed into his chest, sending a different kind of sensation straight to his groin, but Milton redirected his thoughts and smirked. This kind of attack was easy to subvert. He jammed his hands between them and pushed hard on nerves that ran along the insides of both her legs. Her flesh felt wonderful beneath his fingers. Warm and pliant, with cords of muscle running beneath.

Can't think about that, either.

She yelped, and her legs loosened. Encouraged because he was winning, Milton levered her arms from around him, and she slid to the ground, dancing back out of his reach. Color splotched her face, and her chest heaved with each breath. Damn, she looked amazing! He wanted to pull her against him—up close and personal, but Charity rushed him. He barely twisted out of the way in time, using her momentum to drive her to the ground—again. He angled a leg and kicked gently, catching the side neck in a crucial spot with his foot. If they'd been in true combat, and he'd kicked harder, she'd have been dead. At least she would have been if she were a normal human. He wasn't certain if a blow to that particular nerve bundle would kill these gals.

Long, black hair bounced around Charity as she danced from foot to foot. She shoved it out of green eyes gleaming with enthusiasm. Her body was damn near perfect, just like all the genetically altered women. Though they looked much the same, with dark hair and those clear, emerald eyes, small differences made it possible to tell them apart.

Tall, with lithe, muscled grace, Charity bore down on him once more. She swaggered as if she had all the time in the world, but he wasn't fooled. She was catching her breath. Her body-hugging tights and sports bra under a thin T-shirt didn't leave much to the imagination. Neither did Honor's outfit. Like him, the women trained barefoot. He danced away from Charity's frontal attack, pivoting out of her reach. She made a face at him and cocked her head to one side, clearly considering what to do next.

Charity and Honor were breathing hard, which was small compensation, but it still pleased him. He'd taken the series of injections to make him more like the freaks—genetically modified humans who'd escaped the labs that spawned them seven years before and staged a rebellion—and it had proven a good investment.

The MDs pitched a fit, told him he was too old to risk it, so he'd taken matters into his own hands. Setting up the IVs was a bitch, but he'd managed it. Good thing too, or he'd never have been able to hold his own in combat like this.

Honor came at him from the side and twisted an arm around his shoulders. He slithered out from under her iron grasp, feeling her push for entry into his mind. He slammed up a barrier to keep her out. He needed an edge, and having her intuit his next move by peeking would obliterate any advantage his years of martial arts training conferred.

"Hey!" he protested. "You're cheating."

"Well…" Honor drew back and leaned her hands on her knees sucking air. "If we can't win any other way…"

"I'm with her." Charity draped an arm around her friend. She snorted and raked her hands through hair that had mostly escaped from her braids. "God almighty! I don't get why we can't win. There are two of us, for chrissakes. You may be the head of the CIA, but you're still only one dude."

Milton threw his head back and laughed. He'd more or less caught his breath during their brief break. The women came perilously close to *winning*, but he'd be damned if he'd tell them that. He glanced at the wall clock at the far end of the practice gym. "Lunch time." He clasped his hands together, pushing outward to stretch his back and shoulders. "You're due at the gun range afterward. I know you're not crazy about guns, but you need practice with them."

"So we'll see you tomorrow morning?" Honor asked.

"You got it, ladies." Milton grinned. "Same time, same station. If you're lucky, Glory, Faith, and Hope will wear me out this afternoon, and you'll have one up on me tomorrow."

"Fat fucking chance," Charity muttered.

Her profanity drew another laugh from Milton. "You've picked up bad habits pretty damned fast," he noted.

"Hell!" Honor rolled her eyes. "You should see her drink. The Nameless Ones never let us have liquor."

"They missed the boat on a lot of fronts," Milton said. "Now skedaddle, or you'll be late for weapons training."

The door at the far end of the gym swooshed open, and Roy Kincaid strolled in. "Hey, boss!" He snapped off a mock salute, probably to annoy Milton. Tall and rangy, his coppery hair was dyed black. As usual, it was too long, sweeping his collar. His blue eyes held a mischievous glint, and he wore faded jeans and a black turtleneck, topped by a plaid, flannel lumberman's jacket. It was still winter and colder than hell outside most of the time.

"You're such a pain in the ass, Kincaid," Milton snarled and drew a black long-sleeved T-shirt on over the silver tank top he'd been training in. Next he worked his legs into gray sweats.

"You don't really mean that," Honor chortled, and she and Charity loped the length of the spacious room to disappear out the door Roy entered through.

Milton sidled to a bar bolted to the wall. Once he got there, he tugged a towel off it and wiped sweat from his face and neck. Once the door shut behind the women, he turned to Roy. "They're becoming strong fighters. Forcing them to not use their mental ability was an excellent idea."

"You didn't agree with me at first." Roy met him at the side of the gym. He pulled out a chair and dropped into it. "What made you change your mind?"

"They're women," Milton growled. "No matter what, I figured they'd never be a match for a man." He shook his head and pulled up a second chair, hanging the towel back over the bar before he sat. "Brother, was I ever wrong. Those gals are bitches on wheels."

"They are pretty amazing."

"Never thought I'd end up playing nursemaid to a group of Valkyries," Milton muttered.

Roy quirked a brow. "Is it all that bad?"

Milton adopted half a hangdog look and met Roy's direct blue gaze. "If you ever repeat this, Kincaid, I'll say you're delusional, but I'm enjoying the hell out of it. If the specter of war with those monstrosities wasn't hanging over our heads, I'd be happier than a pig rolling in garbage."

"What I don't get..." Roy narrowed his eyes, "...is how the women can be so awesome, and the genetically altered men such bastards. Nameless Ones my ass. Not only did they have names, but they kept the women under such tight control, I'm surprised they didn't slit the guys' throats while they slept."

"Mmph." Milton steepled his fingers together. "Remember all that data Glory downloaded from one of their computers when she merged with it?"

"How could I forget? Shit! She almost died doing that. I could live the rest of my life without a repeat of that level of drama."

"The genetic modifications had a different impact on the women than the men. They're stronger and much more adaptive—"

"Which is why the men kept them under such strict control," Roy finished for him. "Yeah, yeah, I know all that, but now that I've finally found someone to share my life, I want to take care of those fuckers once and for all."

"Dream on." Milton eyed him speculatively. "I'm glad you and Glory are so well-matched. What do you need? Why'd you hunt me down? Surely not to shoot the shit over current affairs."

Roy's expression turned serious. "I want you to come upstairs and take a look at the map we created. The one with Glory's information about the location of all the compounds like the one she and the other women came from."

"Say more." Milton crooked two fingers at Roy.

"Lights are coming on like crazy all across the board. It appears the majority of the compounds are mobilizing. If there's a critical mass they need to accomplish anything, they have to be damned close to it."

"Crap! They're gearing up for something major."

"Unfortunately, it looks that way." Roy frowned. "I'd hoped we could hit a few more compounds and add more women to our special unit, but I doubt we'll have that kind of time."

"Maybe we will. There's a compound not far from here. We could be battle-ready by tonight. The women have trained for a few weeks. It's enough since we'll be with them, along with your team."

"Come look at the map first." Roy pushed to his feet. "Then we'll decide."

"We?"

Roy made a rude sound. "You, boss. I meant you." Another rude blat sounded. "It's actually a relief. I wouldn't take your job if they offered it to me trimmed in diamonds."

"Smart ass." Milton paced Roy the length of the arena and continued to walk next to him out the door, and up the elevator to ground level.

"You're pretty quiet," Roy observed.

"How's Glory dealing with the destruction of her compound? Any guilt for playing an elemental part in leveling the only home she remembers?"

"It took a while, but she's okay with it now." Roy hesitated. "She's still sad the rest of the women in her dorm didn't trust her enough to come with her, but she's more than ready to co-opt other women into joining us in fighting the men. If there's one thing all the women have in common, it's their deep hatred for the Nameless Ones."

"Must be universal from compound to compound."

Roy stopped dead, considering Milton's statement. "I assumed it was, but in truth, I have no idea. Neither would the women since they were so isolated."

They stood near the middle of Langley's enormous campus in a sleeting rain under leaden skies, getting wetter by the moment. Milton grabbed Roy's arm and yanked. "We can debate that from inside." He broke into a run and headed for the building that housed his office and most of their computer systems with Roy hard on his heels.

Milton skipped the elevator and pounded up four flights of stairs, shaking water off as he ran.

"It wouldn't kill you to take the elevator," Roy said from behind him.

"You're getting soft, Kincaid." Milton placed his palm on the scanner and opened the stairwell door that led to his suite of offices. Once he was in the hall, he turned to shoot a significant glance at his old friend. "Or maybe you just need more sleep."

"If you're inferring Glory and I entertain each other every night, you'd be absolutely right." Roy slugged him in the shoulder. "You should try it. When's the last time you got laid?"

Milton tried for a serious face, but couldn't pull it off. "That's not an appropriate question for your superior officer."

"Oh, so it's okay for you to mention my sex life, but not the other way around?"

"Stuff it, Kincaid." Milton pushed into the office beyond his where they'd set up the computer simulation of the compounds, and his good humor evaporated. He walked to the wall mounted map and stared at all the flaring lights in disbelief.

"Pretty sobering, huh?" Roy made his way to his side.

"When did this happen?" Milton pointed at the map. "I've been in the gym with the women since right after breakfast."

"Sometime between last night and this morning. Shit!" Roy tapped the display. "There's another one. That's number twenty. I counted before I came to find you."

Milton unclenched his jaw. "Do you suppose they figured out some way to mimic mobilization? They've likely guessed what Glory did, and their database brains would assume we've come up with a geographic simulation of their locations."

Roy creased his forehead into grim lines. "I have no fucking idea, but I like your explanation better than the other one."

"Which is they're gunning for us in real time. Probably not just us, either. Christ! I wonder what the collateral damage will be to civilians."

"Yeah." Roy's frown deepened. "It's what I'd do in their place. Strike fast and hard. It's been nearly a month since we blew up Glory's compound. I've been expecting them to do something before now."

"I have too." Milton stripped off his wet top and went to a closet in the back of the room where he got a navy blue sweat shirt emblazoned with the CIA's logo and pulled it over his head. He walked back to the map, studying it.

"Look here." He ran his finger over a spot on the map. "This is the compound I'd thought to target next. It's close, just over the West Virginia line not far from Keyser."

"Well." Roy drew out the word. "At least it's not lit up like a fucking Christmas tree." He paused a beat. "Seems odd. They must know where the women are. It should be one of the first to mobilize."

"That'd be logical." Milton slapped his hand on a nearby table. "Adds credibility to my theory that maybe they're fucking with us by creating the illusion they're sending thousands of super humans on the warpath."

Roy turned to face his boss. "It's your call. What do you want to do?"

"I have a few competing ideas I need to work through. Call your team in for a briefing at thirteen hundred hours."

"What about Honor and Charity? Aren't they due at the munitions range then?"

Milton turned it over in his mind. "Maybe we just want your core team at first. In case there are some hard decisions to make."

Emotion played over Roy's face, but he didn't say anything.

"Spit out whatever it is." Milton made come along motions with two fingers.

Roy squared his shoulders. "The women see themselves as your team. You set things up that way to get Glory out from under a direct line of command to me. They're not going to like it if you don't include them in something big like this."

"I'll take it under advisement. Was there anything else?"

Roy smirked. "You never did like having your decisions questioned. Nope. I'm out of here. If you need me, I'll be in my office. And I'll muster my part of the troops for that thirteen hundred meeting."

Milton watched the door shut behind Roy before he perched on the edge of a chair and studied the map some more. At least no new lights started blinking. What did it mean? Were the men in those locations truly getting ready to move against them? What did they have in mind? Mental warfare? Chemical assaults? Or something more prosaic—like bombs?

He scrubbed the heels of his hands down his face, wishing to hell he had better intel. Or that some of the biochemists and genetic engineers who'd developed the mutant humans were available. They were among the first killed when the freaks, sick to death of being experimental targets, rose against their masters and escaped the breeding farms to set up their own compounds. In the intervening time, they'd engaged in small scale guerilla warfare against the government, but nothing major.

Apparently, that was all about to change.

After a last look at the map, he made his way out the door and down the hallway to his office, where he got a sandwich out of the refrigerator. He ate standing up, looking out the window at the Langley campus. He'd headed up the CIA for the last fifteen years. Compared with his early years in Vietnam's steamy jungles, this life was easy. Or it had been. At least in Vietnam, he'd been a solo operative. If he fucked up, the only one who bought it was him.

If he guessed wrong about what the freaks were up to now, tens of thousands of innocent people could die. He took a bite of air and realized he'd finished his sandwich. A glance at the clock told him he had half an hour before meeting with Roy and his men. What about the women? Should he include them?

Milton shut his eyes. The vision that formed behind his lids was Honor wrapped around his body, the heat of her and her decidedly female scent surrounding him right along with her legs. Roy's flip question about when he'd been laid last rose to taunt him. He hadn't had sex in months—maybe as much as a year. When you cut to the chase, he was married to the CIA, and she was a jealous mistress. No other woman had been able to stand up to the demands work placed on him, and after three failed marriages, he'd decided it was better not to go that route again.

Thank fucking God he'd never had any kids. Especially sons. They'd have idolized him, wanted to follow his footsteps into danger, and there would've been one more domestic blowup just waiting to slap him in the face. He understood women. They guarded their offspring with the energy and single-mindedness of a lioness protecting her kill. If anything happened to the sons he'd never had because they were adrenaline junkies like him, he'd never have heard the end of it.

He forced his eyes open, pushed himself to focus. The last thing he needed right now was a trip into the emotional side he kept tightly shuttered. No wives. No kids. He aimed to keep it that way.

Milton turned away from the window and paced from one end of his roomy office to the other as he thought about their next move. Too bad he couldn't find one of the male freaks and convince him to become a double agent. That scenario would provide a ready source of the intel he lacked.

Another glance at the clock told him he had five minutes. Maybe what Roy said about the women being furious if he left them out was right on. If anyone would know, he would, since he and Glory were married all but for the ceremony. Maybe there was something they'd missed in all the data Glory downloaded from the computer in her compound just before Roy blew the place to kingdom come.

Maybe I just want to see Honor again—before tomorrow morning's practice session.

The thought brought him up short, and he gave himself a sharp mental slap. When he started putting his needs above those of The

Company—never mind the American public—it was time to either rearrange his priorities or move on.

He was out of time. Not quite trusting his motives, he picked up the phone on his desk. Once he had it in hand, he dialed the gun range and told the agent to send the women back to the meeting room down the hall from his office.

www.ingramcontent.com/pod-product-compliance
Lightning Source LLC
Chambersburg PA

48292CB00007B/2624